喚醒你的英文語感！

Get a Feel for English !

喚醒你的英文語感！

Get a Feel for English !

從聽不懂到流利對談的學習奇蹟！

職場英文進化術

作者：商英教父 Quentin Brand

Listening • Speaking

菁英篇

Upgrade Your Biz English

貝塔語言出版 Beta Multimedia Publishing
IRT 語言測驗中心 Language Testing Center

目錄 CONTENTS

Unit 1

前 言

收聽廣播或收看電視新聞是獲取全球和國內最新商業訊息的有效方法。如果你收聽的是英文廣播和新聞，這更是你提升英文的最佳方式。本書的設計就是要協助各位聽懂英文新聞、獲取最新商業資訊，進而開口談論相關議題。

一般人聽英文最常犯的錯誤就是專注在他們不懂的部分。這是再自然不過的事，不過，如果你能改變思維，你的聽力就能大幅進步。專注在你懂的部分，可以讓聽英文變得容易！閱讀本書的時候，請時時提醒自己這一點，你就能夠有所體會。

取材

- 本書主題全部取材於商業人士所關注的眞實情境與時事。如果你收聽廣播或收看新聞，這些都是常見主題。
- 本書大致分爲四部分。第一部分：無時間主題（如：公司介紹、事實陳述）；第二部分：現在時間主題（如：當前的市場趨勢）；第三部分：過去時間主題（如：公司歷史、新聞報導）；第四部分：未來時間主題（如：市場預測）。
- 除上述部分，還有兩則訪談，幫助各位聽懂問題並學習應答技巧。

單元設計

- 每一章的單元設計都有學習進程的順序安排，請不要跳著閱讀。閱讀每一章大約需要 90 分鐘，最好可以挪出時間完成每一章，不被打斷。
- 每一章開頭的聽力練習，是測試對該主題的整體理解。我建議你，聽之前先稍微想想你對於該主題有哪些了解。以這種方式活絡已知的知識，有助你理解基本要點。

■ 接著是一些專注在內容細節的練習，包括聽取字彙、俚語和文法。每一章都會精選該主題的關鍵字彙，奠定各位的學習基礎。進而幫助各位學會在上下文中使用它們。

■ 接著，各位會練習字彙發音。研究指出藉由練習發音，可以有效提升聽力。請各位利用 CD 來做聽、說練習，不要忽略它們。

■ 每一章最後是成果驗收的練習，你必須運用在該章所學到的用語，爲聽力段落做個總結並練習說出來。你可以錄音來掌握自己的進步狀況。

■ 每一章都會請各位自我評量，如下：

0% 10% 20% 30% 40% 50% 60% 70% 80% 90% 100%

每章開頭的第一個聽力練習，會請各位在評分線上標示出理解程度。經過一連串字彙、發音、聽力的學習，到了每章的完結，會請各位再次評量對於同一聽力段落的理解。藉由比較二次評分，各位可以清楚看出進步狀況。

■ 你可以依序閱讀本書，或是從你感興趣或最需要加強的單元著手。無論是哪一種方式，請有耐心地讀完每一個章節，如此，你的聽、說能力才會眞正進步。

最後，請記住，專注在你懂的部分，而不是不懂的部分。

祝收聽愉快！

Unit 2

Abercrombie and Fitch

服裝品牌 A&F

學習重點 公司介紹

聽聽看

1 請聽一段關於 Abercrombie and Fitch 服飾公司的介紹，你可以聽懂多少呢？在聽之前，請看看下列字彙，你覺得哪些字會出現在這段聽力中呢。 Track 02

- ☐ accessories 配件
- ☐ church 教堂
- ☐ clothes 服飾
- ☐ counterfeit 仿冒品
- ☐ equipment 設備
- ☐ newspaper 報紙
- ☐ priest 神父
- ☐ professor 教授
- ☐ religious 宗教的
- ☐ textile 織物

小叮嚀

藉由這些單字提示，對你聽懂這段公司介紹是否有幫助呢？請在下列線段標示出你的理解程度，在本章最後，我們會再次做相同的評量，看看你進步了多少。

0% 10% 20% 30% 40% 50% 60% 70% 80% 90% 100%

聽聽看

2 請再聽一次 A&F 的公司介紹，以下的陳述如果「正確」，請標示 T；「錯誤」者請標示 F。 Track 02

例	公司歷史悠久。	T
1	A&F 集團旗下有五家公司。	
2	分店遍及全球，也可於線上購物。	
3	目標客戶為中年階層。	
4	公司備受爭議。	
5	公司出版了一份關於流行產業的報紙。	
6	公司深受基督徒和家庭擁護團體歡迎。	

7	公司服裝在美國某些大學被禁穿。	
8	公司愈來愈不受歡迎。	
9	公司面臨民眾賣假貨的問題。	

答案 請見 19 頁。

如果聽第一次時無法完全掌握上述訊息，請多練習幾次。接著，我們來學習介紹服飾公司時會用到的詞彙。

動動腦 **3 連連看，請將下列字彙與正確意思配對。見範例。**

■ casual clothes •	• 廣告宣傳
■ previous customers •	• 服飾零售商
■ flagship namesake stores •	• 休閒服飾
■ apparel retailers •	• 大學生
■ college students •	• 名牌贗品
■ young graduates •	• 同名旗艦店
■ ad campaigns •	• 生活類雜誌
■ short-run products •	• 過去的顧客
■ lifestyle magazine •	• 情色內容
■ sexual content •	• 短期商品
■ youth market •	• 年輕畢業生
■ fake brand products •	• 年輕人市場

答案 請見 19 頁。核對完答案，請花點時間熟悉這些字彙，並跟著 CD 練習發音。 Track 03

請再回頭聽一次公司介紹，並留意上列字彙在上下文的使用方式，如有需要可以參閱本章末的CD內容，將聽力段落當成字彙的使用範文來學習。

動動腦 **4** 注意到了嗎，在這段公司介紹中使用了一個俚語 come under fire for sth.，其意思為何？請勾選最貼切的解釋。

	come under fire for sth.
	get burned in a fire
	be criticized for sth.
	lose your job

答案 如果摸不著頭緒，可以藉由聽力段落的上下文，判斷此俚語所指為何。答案請見20頁。

現在我們來看看公司介紹所會用到的簡單文法。在這段聽力當中，大部分的動詞都是現在簡單式，因爲陳述的內容大部分是關於A&F公司的一些「事實」。

動動腦 **5** 請用下列動詞填空，完成句子。有些動詞不只使用一次。

be	**forbid**	**have**	**own**
print	**remain**	**sell**	**target**

1. A&F ________ upscale men's, women's, and kids' casual clothes.
2. The company ________ a long history.

3. A&F ________ 1,000-plus stores.

4. It also ________ abercrombie kids.

5. The company ________ college students.

6. Some of the logos and slogans the company prints on its t-shirts ________ also controversial.

7. Some Christian universities and schools in the US ________ their students to wear the company's clothes.

8. The company's products ________ very fashionable.

9. Counterfeiting of their products ________ a big problem.

答案 請見 20 頁。請留意動詞與主詞的一致性。

另外需要注意的是，在這段公司介紹中有兩個被動式的字串：

- **be criticized for sth.** 因……而遭受批評
- **sth. be produced** ……被生產

動動腦 **6 請使用正確的 be 動詞形式完成下列句子。**

1. Its lifestyle magazine *A&F Quarterly* ________ often criticized.

2. Many fake brand products ________ produced and sold.

答案 請見 20 頁。請留意 be 動詞和主詞的一致性，單數主詞搭配 is；複數主詞則使用 are。

說說看

7 請使用你在本章學會的字彙和文法，為這段公司介紹做個摘要，並練習開口說。

小叮嚀

請把你的口說摘要錄音，並聽錄音評量自己的進步狀況。可以多練習幾次，直到可以說得流利。

聽聽看

8 最後請再聽一次 **A&F** 的公司介紹，並在下列線段標示出你的理解程度。經過一連串學習，你的聽力理解進步了嗎？如果沒有，請再回頭針對弱項加強。 Track 02

0% 10% 20% 30% 40% 50% 60% 70% 80% 90% 100%

解答

聽聽看 2

1. T
2. T
3. F，目標客戶是大學生和兒童。
4. T
5. F，出版的是生活類雜誌。
6. F，這些團體經常批評公司。
7. T
8. F，公司一直很受歡迎。
9. T

動動腦 3

casual clothes	休閒服飾
previous customers	過去的顧客
flagship namesake stores	同名旗艦店
apparel retailers	服飾零售商
college students	大學生
young graduates	年輕畢業生
ad campaigns	廣告宣傳
short-run products	短期商品
lifestyle magazine	生活類雜誌
sexual content	情色內容
youth market	年輕人市場
fake brand products	名牌贗品

動動腦 4

come under fire for sth. = **be criticized for sth.** 因某事而遭批評

動動腦 5

1. A&F **sells** upscale men's, women's, and kids' casual clothes.
2. The company **has** a long history.
3. A&F **has** 1,000-plus stores.
4. It also **owns** abercrombie kids.
5. The company **targets** college students.
6. Some of the logos and slogans the company prints on its t-shirts **are** also controversial.
7. Some Christian universities and schools in the US **forbid** their students to wear the company's clothes.
8. The company's products **remain** very fashionable.
9. Counterfeiting of their products **remains** a big problem.

動動腦 6

1. Its lifestyle magazine *A&F Quarterly* **is** often criticized.
2. Many fake brand products **are** produced and sold.

CD 內容

Track 02

Abercrombie and Fitch, or A and F, sells upscale men's, women's, and kids' casual clothes and accessories. The company has a long history of selling travel and safari clothes and equipment to the rich and famous. Its previous customers include Hemingway, Steinbeck and Teddy Roosevelt.

A and F has 1,000-plus stores in North America (mostly in malls) and also sells through its catalog and online. In addition to its flagship namesake stores, it also owns abercrombie kids, Hollister Co, Ruehl No.925 and Gilly Hicks, all apparel retailers. The company targets college students, young graduates and urbanites, and kids.

It has come under fire for some of its ad campaigns, as well as for some of its short-run products. For example, its lifestyle magazine *A and F Quarterly* is often criticized by religious and family groups for the sexual content of its pictures and articles. And some of the logos and slogans the company prints on its t-shirts are also controversial. Some Christian universities and schools in the US forbid their students from wearing the company's clothes.

Despite this, the company's products remain very popular with the youth market. In fact, counterfeiting of their products remains a big problem for the company in Asia, where many fake brand products are produced and sold.

【中譯】

Abercrombie and Fitch（或 A&F）銷售高級男士、女士和兒童休閒服飾與配件。富豪名流購買該公司旅行服飾和用品的歷史悠久，過去的顧客包括有海明威、斯坦貝克與羅斯福總統。

A&F 在北美擁有一千家以上的店面（大部分位於購物中心內），還有郵購與線上購物的銷售管道。除了同名旗艦店之外，還擁有 abercrombie kids、Hollister Co、Ruehl No.925 和 Gilly Hicks 所有的服飾零售商。該公司的目標客戶是大學生、年輕畢業生、都市族，以及兒童。

該公司的廣告宣傳和一些短期產品曾遭受批評。舉例來說，它的生活類雜誌《A and F 季刊》就常因情色內容、照片和文章而遭到宗教與家庭擁護團體抨擊。公司印在 T 恤商品上的某些標語和口號也引發爭議，一些美國的基督教大學和學院禁止他們的學生穿著這家公司的服飾。

儘管如此，該公司的產品依然受到年輕人市場的歡迎。事實上，亞洲地區的商品仿冒問題一直是該公司的一大困擾，在該地區有諸多名牌膺品的生產和銷售。

Unit 3

Unemployment Has Risen to 7.5%.

失業率攀升至 7.5% 。

學習重點 就業市場

聽聽看

1 請聽一段關於就業市場的報導，你可以聽懂多少呢？在聽之前，請看看下列字彙，你覺得哪些字會出現在這段聽力當中呢。 Track 04

- ☐ economy 經濟
- ☐ job 工作
- ☐ professor 教授
- ☐ staff 職員
- ☐ vacancy 職缺
- ☐ industry 產業
- ☐ price 價格
- ☐ shopping 購物
- ☐ student 學生
- ☐ women 女性

小叮嚀

藉由這些單字提示，對你聽懂這段報導是否有幫助呢？請在下列線段標示出你的理解程度，在本章最後，我們會再次做相同的評量，看看你進步了多少。

0% 10% 20% 30% 40% 50% 60% 70% 80% 90% 100%

聽聽看

2 請再聽一次這段就業市場的報導，以下陳述如果「正確」，請標示 **T**；「錯誤」者請標示 **F**。 Track 04

例	新聞報導是關於就業市場。	T
1	政府發布了一份報告。	
2	報告是關於失業數據。	
3	報告描述了目前情況。	
4	網路上的徵才廣告減少。	
5	每個公司都迅速遞補離職員工的職缺。	
6	每個公司都不聘雇新員工。	

7	失業率攀升。	
8	民眾愈來愈容易找到工作。	
9	所有類型的工作都受到不景氣影響。	

答案 請見29頁。

如果聽第一次時無法完全掌握上述訊息，請多練習幾次。接著，我們來學習和就業市場相關的用語。

動動腦 **3** 連連看，請將下列字彙與正確意思配對。見範例。

■ business growth •	• 徵才廣告
■ issued a report •	• 工作職缺
■ job adverts •	• 發佈一份報告
■ job recruitment agencies •	• 員工需求
■ job vacancies •	• 謀得新職
■ staffing needs •	• 業務成長
■ workloads •	• 登錄職缺
■ advertised vacancies •	• 人力仲介商
■ find new positions •	• 高薪管理工作
■ food service jobs •	• 工作量
■ high paying management jobs •	• 運輸工作
■ transport jobs •	• 大幅下滑
■ very sharp decline •	• 餐飲服務工作

答案 請見29頁。核對完答案，請花點時間熟悉這些字彙，並跟著CD練習發音。 Track 05

請再回頭聽一次就業市場的報導，並留意上列字彙在上下文的使用方式，如有需要可以參閱本章末的 CD 內容，將聽力段落當成字彙的使用範文來學習。

動動腦 **4** **注意到了嗎，在這段就業市場報導中使用了一個俚語 pick up the slack，其意思為何？請勾選最貼切的解釋。**

	pick up the slack
	find something you lost earlier
	pick something up from the ground
	get lazy
	do the work which someone else has stopped doing, but which still needs to be done

答案 如果摸不著頭緒，可以藉由聽力段落的上下文，判斷此俚語所指為何。答案請見 30 頁。

現在讓我們來看看在就業市場報導中所使用的動詞時態。

動動腦 **5** **如果要將下列動詞分成兩類，你會如何分類？**

- have received
- have reduced
- are not hiring
- are not looking to
- are asking
- are increasing
- have stopped growing
- has slowed
- has risen
- is making

答案 請見 30 頁。

分析

- 希望你能看出這些動詞字串大致可分成：have + p.p. 和 be Ving 二類。
- 這則報導描述的是就業市場的目前情況。
- Have + p.p. 動詞字串表達的是一個現在的結果；be Ving 動詞字串表達的則是一個目前的活動，或是一種當前的趨勢，無關乎結果。

聽聽看

6 請再聽一次報導，並依序將下列字串的主詞填上（如果有受詞或副詞，也請填上）。 Track 04

1. ________ have received ________________
2. ________ have reduced ________________
3. ________ are not hiring ________________
4. ________ are not looking to ________________
5. ________ are asking ________________
6. ________ are increasing ________________
7. ________ have stopped growing ________________
8. ________ has slowed ________________
9. ________ has risen ________________
10. ________ is making ________________

答案 請見 30 頁。核對完答案，請花點間看看這些動詞字串如何用來談論就業市場的現況。

說說看

7 請使用你在本章學會的字彙和文法，為這段就業市場報導做個摘要，並練習開口說。

小叮嚀

請把你的口說摘要錄音，並聽錄音評量自己的進步狀況。可以多練習幾次，直到可以說得流利。

聽聽看

8 最後請再聽一次就業市場報導，並在下列線段標示出你的理解程度。經過一連串學習，你的聽力理解進步了嗎？如果沒有，請再回頭針對弱項加強。 Track 04

0%　10%　20%　30%　40%　50%　60%　70%　80%　90%　100%

解答

聽聽看 2

1. F，報告是由兩家網路人力仲介公司發布的。
2. F，報告是關於網路工作職缺。
3. T
4. T
5. F，每個公司都不遞補離職員工的職缺。
6. T
7. T
8. F，民眾愈來愈難找到工作。
9. T

動動腦 3

business growth	業務成長
issued a report	發布一份報告
job adverts	徵才廣告
job recruitment agencies	人力仲介商
job vacancies	工作職缺
staffing needs	員工需求
workloads	工作量
advertised vacancies	登錄職缺
find new positions	謀得新職
food service jobs	餐飲服務工作
high paying management jobs	高薪管理工作
transport jobs	運輸工作
very sharp decline	大幅下滑

動動腦 4

pick up the slack = **do the work which someone else has stopped doing, but which still needs to be done** 接手他人做到一半但仍須完成的工作

動動腦 5

這些動詞字串大致可分成：**have + p.p.** 和 **be Ving** 二類。

聽聽看 6

1. **They** have received **fewer job adverts**.
2. **Companies** have reduced **their staffing needs**.
3. **They** are not hiring **more people**.
4. **Companies** are not looking to **replace staff**.
5. **They** are asking **staff to work harder**.
6. **Workloads** are increasing.
7. **Companies** have stopped growing.
8. **Business growth** has slowed.
9. **Unemployment** has risen **to 7.5%**.
10. **The sharp decline in job vacancies** is making **it hard to find new jobs**.

CD 內容

Track 04

And now some more bad news for the job market. Two of the biggest online job recruitment agencies, careerbuild.com and monster.com, issued a report yesterday saying that advertised job vacancies fell sharply in January.

Both sites said that they have received fewer job adverts in the last month. This means that companies have reduced their staffing needs, and that they are not hiring more people. Analysts said there might be two reasons for this: one is that companies are not looking to replace staff who leave. Instead, they are asking staff to work harder and pick up the slack. Most workloads across all industries are increasing. Another reason is that companies have simply stopped growing. Business growth has slowed over the last two quarters, which means that companies have no need to hire more staff.

This is bad news for the economy as it means unemployment has risen to 7.5%. The very sharp decline in advertised vacancies throughout the nation in the last two months is clearly making it increasingly hard for those who are unemployed to find new positions. In Michigan state, the worst hit, there are roughly 6 people competing for every advertised job. The drop in job vacancies extends across all job types, from high paying management jobs, to low paying transport and food service jobs.

【中譯】

現在關於就業市場還有一些壞消息。最大的兩家網路人力仲介商careerbuild.com和monster.com昨天發布一份報告，指出一月份登錄的工作職缺大幅下滑。

兩家網站皆表示上個月所接到的徵才廣告減少，這表示公司已經縮減他們的員工需求，停止聘雇更多的人。據專家分析，此種情況有兩個可能原因：其一是公司不打算找人遞補離職員工，反而要求員工更賣力並接手這些工作。所有產業的工作量大部分都增加了。另一個原因是公司乾脆停止擴充。過去兩季的業務成長緩慢，也就是說公司沒有必要雇用更多員工。

這對經濟來說是壞消息，因為這表示失業率已經攀升至7.5%。過去兩個月全國各地登錄的職缺大幅下滑，顯然會讓目前失業的民眾更加難以謀得新職。在影響最劇的密西根州，每項登錄的工作大約都有六個人競爭。工作職缺減少的情況遍及所有工作類型，從高薪管理工作到低薪的運輸和餐飲服務工作皆然。

Unit 4

99 Cents Only Inc.

僅九十九分有限公司

學習重點 財務報告（英國口音）

聽聽看

1 請聽一段 99 Cents Only Inc. 的財務報告，你可以聽懂多少呢？在聽之前，請看看下列字彙，你覺得哪些字會出現在這段聽力中呢。 Track 06

- ☐ cooking 烹調
- ☐ jump 跳
- ☐ money 錢
- ☐ retailer 零售商
- ☐ share 股份
- ☐ subsidiary 子公司
- ☐ trade 貿易
- ☐ transport 運輸
- ☐ wholesaler 批發商
- ☐ workers 工人

小叮嚀

藉由這些單字提示，對你聽懂這段財務報告是否有幫助呢？請在下列線段標示出你的理解程度，在本章最後，我們會再次做相同的評量，看看你進步了多少。

0% 10% 20% 30% 40% 50% 60% 70% 80% 90% 100%

聽聽看

2 請再聽一次這段財務報告，以下陳述如果「正確」，請標示 T；「錯誤」者請標示 F。 Track 06

例	公司擁有兩家子公司。	T
1	公司主要銷售高價商品。	
2	財務報告是關於去年第三季。	
3	公司當季的獲利增加了 31%。	
4	當季的所得是 1,250 萬美金。	
5	當季的業績是 3 億 2,500 萬美金。	

6	支出減少。	
7	成長的業績大多是來自 Bargain Wholesale 子公司。	
8	公司的股價下跌了 0.06 美元。	

答案 請見 39 頁。

如果聽第一次時無法完全掌握上述訊息，請多練習幾次。接著，我們來學習談論財務狀況時會用到的字彙。

動動腦 **3 連連看，請將下列字彙與正確意思配對。見範例。**

■ discount retailer •	• 連鎖商店
■ fiscal third-quarter profit •	• 折扣零售店
■ namesake chain •	• 折扣商店
■ retail subsidiaries •	• 會計年度第三季獲利
■ chain of stores •	• 高折扣價格
■ wholesale products •	• 同名連鎖店
■ greatly discounted prices •	• 淨所得
■ discount stores •	• 零售子公司
■ net income •	• 批發商品

答案 請見 39 頁。核對完答案，請花點時間熟悉這些字彙，並跟著 CD 練習發音。 Track 07

請再回頭聽一次財務報告，並留意上列字彙在上下文的使用方式，如有需要可以參閱本章末的 CD 內容，將聽力段落當成字彙的使用範文來學習。

談論財務相關的資訊，免不了需要提及許多數據，能夠習慣「聽」和「說」數字是一項重要技能。接著，我們就來做這方面的練習。

說說看

4 請聽 CD，並跟著練習這些數字的發音。

Track 08

- 31 percent（31 個百分點）
- 280
- 18 cents（18 分）
- 14 cents（14 分）
- $351.1 million（3 億 5,110 萬美元）
- $125.9 million（1 億 2,590 萬美元）
- 2 percent（2 個百分點）
- 6 cents（6 分）
- $5.37（5.37 美元）
- 52 weeks（52 週）
- 99 cents（99 分）
- $12.5 million（1,250 萬美元）
- $9.5 million（950 萬美元）
- 8 percent（8 個百分點）
- $325 million（3 億 2,500 萬美元）
- $118.3 million（1 億 1,830 萬美元）
- $252,000（25 萬 2 千元）
- $8.13（8.13 美元）
- $12.86（12.86 美元）

熟悉了這些數字的發音，可以做點小測試，請回頭再聽一次財務報導，你可以在上下文中清楚聽出這些數字資訊嗎？如果不行，請再多練習幾次。

說說看

5 有時候所提及的不是精確數據，而是概數，那麼你就會需要下列表示「大概」的用語。請利用 CD 練習發音。

Track 09

- in part 部分
- about 大約
- partly 部分
- roughly 大概

聽聽看 **6** 請再聽一次財務報告，並將你所聽到表示「大概」的用語填入下列句子。 Track 06

1. … due __________ to a jump in sales ...
2. A chain of stores which sells wholesale products at __________ discounted prices ...
3. The company operates __________ 280 discount stores ...
4. The stock traded between __________ $5.37 and $12.86 ...

答案 請見 39 頁。核對完答案，請花點時間熟悉「大概」用語在上下文的使用方式。

這篇財務報告所談論的是「過去」的業績表現，所以每一個描述財務狀況的動詞都是使用簡單過去式。

說說看 **7** 下列是談論財務狀況最常使用的動作詞彙，請跟著 CD 練習發音。 Track 10

- rise 、 rose 、 risen 增加；上揚
- fall 、 fell 、 fallen 減少；下跌
- post 、 posted 、 posted 公告；宣布
- a jump in sth. 某物暴增
- a drop in sth. 某物暴跌

聽聽看

8 請再聽一次財務報告，並利用上一題的詞彙完成下列句子。 Track 06

1. Fiscal third-quarter profit ____________ 31 percent.
2. The company ____________ a net income of $12.5 million.
3. Sales ____________ 8 percent.
4. Expenses ____________ to $125.9 million.
5. ... the ____________ in sales.
6. Sales ____________ about 2 percent.
7. Shares ____________ 6 cents.

答案 請見 40 頁。核對完答案，請花點時間熟悉這些動作詞彙在上下文的使用方式。

說說看

9 請使用你在本章學會的用語，為這段財務報告做個摘要，並練習開口說。

小叮嚀

請把你的口說摘要錄音，並聽錄音評量自己的進步狀況。可以多練習幾次，直到能夠說得流利。

聽聽看

10 最後請再聽一次財務報告，並在下列線段標示出你的理解程度。經過一連串學習，你的聽力理解進步了嗎？如果沒有，請再回頭針對弱項加強。 Track 06

0% 10% 20% 30% 40% 50% 60% 70% 80% 90% 100%

解答

聽聽看 2

1. F，公司主要銷售低價商品。
2. T
3. T
4. T
5. F，業績是 3 億 5,100 萬美元。
6. F，支出增加。
7. F，成長的業績大多是來自 99 Cents Only 子公司。
8. T

動動腦 3

discount retailer	折扣零售商
fiscal third-quarter profit	會計年度第三季獲利
namesake chain	同名連鎖店
retail subsidiaries	零售子公司
chain of stores	連鎖商店
wholesale products	批發商品
greatly discounted prices	高折扣價格
discount stores	折扣商店
net income	淨所得

聽聽看 6

1. ... due <u>in part</u> to a jump in sales ...
2. A chain of stores which sells wholesale products at <u>partly</u> discounted prices ...
3. The company operates <u>about</u> 280 discount stores ...

4. The stock traded between **roughly** $5.37 and $12.86 ...

聽聽看 8

1. Fiscal third-quarter profit **rose** 31 percent.
2. The company **posted** a net income of $12.5 million.
3. Sales **rose** 8 percent.
4. Expenses **rose** to $125.9 million.
5. ... the **jump** in sales.
6. Sales **fell** about 2 percent.
7. Shares **fell** 6 cents.

CD 內容

Track 06

Discount retailer 99 Cents Only Stores said Wednesday its fiscal third-quarter profit rose 31 percent due in part to a jump in sales at its namesake chain. The company owns two retail subsidiaries: 99 Cents Only Stores, in which all goods are sold for 99 cents, and Bargain Wholesale, a chain of stores which sells wholesale products at partly discounted prices. The company operates about 280 discount stores throughout California, Texas, Arizona and Nevada.

For the three-month period ended in Dec. 27, the company posted a net income of $12.5 million, or 18 cents per share, compared with $9.5 million, or 14 cents per share, in the year-earlier period.

Sales rose 8 percent to $351.1 million from $325 million.

Expenses rose to $125.9 million from $118.3 million.

The jump in sales was due to the company's 99 Cents Only Stores. Sales fell about 2 percent, or $252,000, at the Bargain Wholesale store chain.

Shares fell 6 cents to close Wednesday at $8.13. The stock traded between roughly $5.37 and $12.86 last year.

【中譯】

折扣零售商 99 Cents Only Stores 週三表示，公司的會計年度第三季獲利增加了 31% ，部分歸因於同名連鎖店的業績暴增。公司擁有兩家零售子公司：99 Cents Only Stores ，這家公司所有商品的售價都是 0.99 塊美金；以及 Bargain Wholesale ，這是一家以部分折扣價銷售批發產品的連鎖商店。公司大約經營了 280 間的折扣商店，遍及加州、德州、亞歷桑納州和那華達州。

結算至十二月二十七日的三個月期間，公司公布淨利為 1 千 250 萬美元，或每股 0.18 美元，相較於去年同期的 950 萬美元，或每股 0.14 美元。

業績增加 8% ，從 3 億 2 千 500 萬美元到 3 億 5 千 110 萬美元。

支出從 1 億 1 千 830 萬美元增加至 1 億 2 千 590 萬美元。

業績暴增歸因於公司的 99 Cents Only Stores 。而 Bargain Wholesales 連鎖商店的業績則下跌大約 2% ， 25 萬 2 千美元。

股價下跌 0.06 美元，週三收盤在 8.13 美元。去年的股票交易大約在 5.37 美元至 12.86 美元之間。

Unit 5

Amazon Kindle
亞馬遜電子書閱讀器

學習重點 新產品上市

聽聽看

1 請聽一段關於 Amazon 推出新產品的報導，你可以聽懂多少呢？在聽之前，請看看下列字彙，你覺得哪些字會出現在這段聽力中呢。 Track 11

- ☐ author 作者
- ☐ bestseller 暢銷書
- ☐ book 書
- ☐ cover 封面
- ☐ device 裝置
- ☐ electronic 電子的
- ☐ news 新聞
- ☐ price 價格
- ☐ shipping 運送
- ☐ writer 寫者

小叮嚀

藉由這些單字提示，對你聽懂這段報導是否有幫助呢？請在下列線段標示出你的理解程度，在本章最後，我們會再次做相同的評量，看看你進步了多少。

○—○—○—○—○—○—○—○—○—○—○

0% 10% 20% 30% 40% 50% 60% 70% 80% 90% 100%

聽聽看

2 請再聽一次 Amazon 新產品的介紹，以下陳述如果「正確」，請標示 T；「錯誤」者請標示 F。 Track 11

例	這段報導是關於 Amazon 所推出名為 Kindle 的電子閱讀器。	T
1	新機型是第二代的電子閱讀器。	
2	這個機型名為 Kindle 3。	
3	這個機型預計二月 24 日可以出貨。	
4	這個機型的售價將會比第一代閱讀器更高。	
5	新型 Kindle 的厚度是三分之一英吋。	
6	這台閱讀器可以儲存 1 千 5 百本書。	

7	Amazon 在 2008 年售出 5 萬台 Kindle。	
8	Amazon 銷售此種產品已有 14 個月之久。	

答案 請見 49 頁。

如果聽第一次時無法完全掌握上述訊息，請多練習幾次。接著，我們來學習談論新產品上市時會用到的字彙。

動動腦 **3 連連看，請將下列字彙與正確意思配對。見範例。**

■ unveil •	• 電池壽命
■ second-generation version •	• 缺貨
■ electronic reading device •	• 削價
■ battery life •	• 電子閱讀器
■ read text aloud •	• 新發售
■ cut the price •	• 記者會
■ new releases •	• 朗讀文字
■ be out of stock •	• 第二代機型
■ updated device •	• 推出
■ news conference •	• 升級的裝置

答案 請見 49 頁。核對完答案，請花點時間熟悉這些字彙，並跟著 CD 練習發音。 Track 12

請再回頭聽一次公司介紹，並留意上列字彙在上下文的使用方式，如有需要可以參閱本章末的 CD 內容，將聽力段落當成字彙的使用範文來學習。

在談論新品上市時，日期、售價等數字都屬於重要資訊，我們接著來練習這方面的發音和聽力。

說說看 **4 請練習下列數字和日期的發音。** Track 13

- February 24th
- 2007
- 10.2
- 1,500
- $10
- 2008
- $359
- 1/3
- 16
- 200
- 500,000
- 14

在這段新產品上市的報導中使用了 dub 這個字，此動詞有兩個意思，我們來研究一下。

動動腦 **5 下列是 dub 的二種用法，請勾選在這篇報導中 dub 是屬於哪一種用法。**

	dub (v.)
	be dubbed sth. = call sth. by a name
	dub sth. = put another voice in a different language, usually over a TV show or movie

答案 如果摸不著頭緒，可以藉由聽力段落的上下文，判斷 dub 為何意。答案請見 49 頁。

在這則報導中，由於談論的大部分是關於未來的事件，所以使用了許多表達未來的字串。

說說看

6 請研讀下列表達未來的字串，並跟著 CD 練習發音。

Track 14

- is due to V
- is to begin Ving
- will probably V
- will be able to V
- might V
- are expected to V
- is going to V

聽聽看

7 請再聽一次新產品上市的報導，並依序完成下列句子。

Track 11

1. ________________ is due to ________________________________
2. ________________ is to begin ______________________________
3. ________________ will probably ____________________________
4. ________________ will be able to __________________________
5. ________________ might ___________________________________
6. ________________ are expected to __________________________
7. ________________ is going to ______________________________

答案 請見 50 頁。核對完答案，請花點間看看這些字串如何用來談論新產品上市。

說說看

8 請使用你在本章學會的用語，為這段新產品上市報導做個摘要，並練習開口說。

小叮嚀

請把你的口說摘要錄音，並聽錄音評量自己的進步狀況。可以多練習幾次，直到可以說得流利。

聽聽看

9 最後請再聽一次報導，並在下列線段標示出你的理解程度。經過一連串學習，你的聽力理解進步了嗎？如果沒有，請再回頭針對弱項加強。 Track 11

0%　10%　20%　30%　40%　50%　60%　70%　80%　90%　100%

解答

聽聽看 2

1. T
2. F，名為 Kindle 2 。
3. T
4. F，售價相同。
5. T
6. T
7. F，售出 50 萬台。
8. F，此產品多年來一直在銷售，不過業績在 14 個月前才有起色。

動動腦 3

unveil	推出
second-generation version	第二代機型
electronic reading device	電子閱讀器
battery life	電池壽命
read text aloud	朗讀文字
cut the price	削價
new releases	新發售
be out of stock	缺貨
updated device	升級的裝置
news conference	記者會

動動腦 5

be dubbed sth. = **call sth. by a name** 被命名為……

聽聽看 7

1. **Amazon** is due to **unveil the second-generation version**.
2. **The new version** is to begin **shipping on February 24**.
3. **It** will probably **cost $359**.
4. **The new device screen** will be able to **show 16 shades of grey**.
5. **Amazon** might **cut the price**.
6. **Sales for the new version** are expected to **more than double**.
7. **The updated device** is going to **be shown at a New York City news conference**.

CD 内容

Track 11

Amazon is due to unveil the second-generation version of its Kindle electronic reading device, with what the company says are improvements in the display, battery life, and operation of the device.

The new version, dubbed the Kindle 2, is to begin shipping on February 24th. It will probably cost $359, the same as the first-generation device, which was introduced in 2007.

The new Kindle is just over 1/3 of an inch thick and weighs 10.2 ounces. The new device screen will be able to show 16 shades of gray, compared with four on the original Kindle. It can also read text aloud and store 1,500 titles, compared with 200 on the previous version.

Some analysts speculate that Amazon might cut the price of the second-generation reader. Best sellers and new releases in electronic form cost about $10 each from Amazon. The original Kindle has been out of stock at Amazon since late last year. It is estimated that Amazon sold 500,000 kindles in 2008, but sales for the new version are expected to more than double in the year ahead.

The updated device is going to be shown at a New York City news conference by company CEO Jeff Bezos. "We've been working on selling e-books for years, but that didn't work until 14 months ago," Bezos said in a pre-launch statement.

【中譯】

Amazon 預計推出 Kindle 電子閱讀器第二代機型，該公司表示，此機型在顯示器、電池壽命和裝置的操作上都做了改善。

被稱為 Kindle 2 的新機型將於二月 24 日開始出貨，售價大約為 359 美金，和 2007 年問世的第一代機型售價相同。

新型 Kindle 的厚度只有 1/3 英吋多，重量是 10.2 盎司。新型閱讀器的螢幕能夠顯示 16 色灰階，相較於原來的 Kindle 只有 4 色灰階。而且可以朗讀文字和儲存 1,500 本書，相較於前一個版本只有 200 本書。

有些分析家推測 Amazon 可能會調降第二代閱讀器的價格。 Amazon 暢銷書和新書的電子版本售價大約為每本 10 塊美金。原機型的 Kindle 從去年底就開始缺貨，據估 Amazon 在 2008 年售出 50 萬台 Kindle ，不過新機型預計在新年度就會有超過兩倍的銷售量。

升級版閱讀器將會在紐約記者會上由公司執行長 Jeff Bezos 展示。 Bezos 在上市前的聲明稿中表示：「多年來我們一直致力於電子書的銷售，不過一直到 14 個月前才有起色。」

Unit 6

Interview with Dan Welch — Part 1

Dan Welch 訪談錄：第一部分

學習重點 行銷策略

聽聽看

1 請聽一段行銷大師 Dan Welch 的訪談，你可以聽懂多少呢？在聽之前，請看看下列字彙，你覺得哪些字會出現在這段聽力中呢。 Track 15

- ☐ brand image 品牌形象
- ☐ customer 顧客
- ☐ discount 折扣
- ☐ downturn（景氣、物價等）下跌
- ☐ price cutting 削價
- ☐ sale 銷售
- ☐ satisfaction 滿意
- ☐ special offer 特別折扣
- ☐ strategy 策略
- ☐ supplier 供應商

小叮嚀

藉由這些單字提示，對你聽懂這段訪談是否有幫助呢？請在下列線段標示出你的理解程度，在本章最後，我們會再次做相同的評量，看看你進步了多少。

0% 10% 20% 30% 40% 50% 60% 70% 80% 90% 100%

聽聽看

2 請再聽一次訪談，以下陳述如果「正確」，請標示 T；「錯誤」者請標示 F。 Track 15

例	著重服務比著重品牌或產品更為重要。	T
1	好的服務可以提高 25% 的顧客維繫。	
2	好的服務可以縮短 20% 的銷售週期。	
3	這份調查問了三個問題。	
4	第一個問題：持續向供應商進貨的原因為何。	
5	第二個問題：停止進貨的原因為何。	

6	第三個問題：為何會將供應商推薦給他人。	
7	有三個策略。	
8	第一個策略：著重產品。	
9	忠誠度指數是用來評量顧客忠誠度的行銷工具。	

答案 請見59頁。

如果聽第一次時無法完全掌握上述訊息，請多練習幾次。接著，我們來學習談論行銷策略時會用到的字彙。

動動腦 **3** 連連看，請將下列字彙與正確意思配對。見範例。

■ marketing guru •	• 品牌知名度
■ retain customers •	• 有業務往來的客戶
■ service excellence •	• 一般認知
■ customer retention •	• 顧客忠誠度
■ promote a supplier's reputation •	• 客戶維繫
■ business contacts •	• 經濟蕭條
■ down economy •	• 忠誠度指數
■ conventional wisdom •	• 行銷大師
■ customer loyalty •	• 行銷工具
■ product quality •	• 更加注重
■ brand recognition •	• 產品品質
■ place greater emphasis •	• 宣揚供應商的聲譽
■ sales experience •	• 留住客戶
■ loyalty index •	• 銷售體驗
■ marketing tool •	• 優質服務

答案 請見59頁。核對完答案，請花點時間熟悉這些字彙，並跟著CD練習發音。 Track 16

請再回頭聽一次訪談，並留意上列字彙在上下文的使用方式，如有需要可以參閱本章末的CD內容，將聽力段落當成字彙的使用範文來學習。

動動腦 **4** 注意到了嗎，在這段訪談中使用了一個俚語 **contrary to conventional wisdom**，其意思為何？請勾選最貼切的解釋。

	contrary to conventional wisdom
	something which everyone knows
	something which is wise
	something which is different from what everyone thinks

答案 如果摸不著頭緒，可以藉由聽力段落的上下文，判斷此俚語所指為何。答案請見60頁。

接著，來看一些訪談中使用的字串。

動動腦 **5** 如果要將下列字串分成二類，你會怎麼分呢？

- be tied to 被束縛於
- emphasis on 注重在
- focus on 專注在
- pull back 撤退
- satisfaction with 對……滿意
- commit to 致力於
- find out 找出
- listen to 聽
- rely on 依賴
- pleasure to ……的樂趣

答案 請見 60 頁。希望你可以看出它們可分為動詞字串和名詞字串。focus 當名詞用時，則 focus on 可歸類為名詞字串。

聽聽看 **6** 請再聽一次訪談，並以上一題的字串完成這些句子。

Track 15

1. We're going to ________ an interview.
2. My ________ be here.
3. The basic message here is ________ how you sell instead of just ________ the product.
4. The customer is ________.
5. They wanted to ________ what makes them willing to …
6. Customer loyalty is not necessarily ________ just product quality.
7. Customers place significantly greater ________ their ________ the sales experience.
8. They ________ a particular supplier.

答案 請見 60 頁。

動動腦 **7** 請將下列單字重新排列、組合成訪談中的問句。

1. through do retain how the customers you downturn?

____

2. are service focus emphasizing you a on?

____

3. do how the increase you customer when retention pulling customer is back?

____

4. are what strategies those?

____

5. you by what mean that do?

____

6. is loyalty overall an what index?

____

答案 請見60頁。熟悉發問方式，可以幫助你在對談中主動提問，延續對話的進行。

說說看 **8** 請使用你在本章學會的用語，為這段行銷策略訪談做個摘要，並練習開口說。

小叮嚀

請把你的口說摘要錄音，並聽錄音評量自己的進步狀況。可以多練習幾次，直到可以說得流利。

聽聽看 **9** 最後請再聽一次訪談，並在下列線段標示出你的理解程度。經過一連串學習，你的聽力理解進步了嗎？如果沒有，請再回頭針對弱項加強。 **Track 15**

0% — 10% — 20% — 30% — 40% — 50% — 60% — 70% — 80% — 90% — 100%

解答

聽聽看 2

1. F，提高 20%。
2. F，縮短 25%。
3. T
4. T
5. F，問題為：你為何會隨著時間而愈買愈多。
6. T
7. T
8. F，第一個策略為：著重銷售經驗。
9. T

動動腦 3

marketing guru	行銷大師
retain customers	留住客戶
service excellence	優質服務
customer retention	客戶維繫
promote a supplier's reputation	宣揚供應商的聲譽
business contacts	有業務往來的客戶
down economy	經濟蕭條
conventional wisdom	一般認知
customer loyalty	顧客忠誠度
product quality	產品品質
brand recognition	品牌知名度
place greater emphasis	更加注重
sales experience	銷售體驗
loyalty index	忠誠度指數
marketing tool	行銷工具

動動腦 4

contrary to conventional wisdom = **something which is different from what everyone thinks** 與一般認知不同的事物

動動腦 5

這些字串可分為動詞和名詞字串：

- 動詞字串：be tied to、focus on、commit to、find out、listen to、pull back、rely on
- 名詞字串：emphasis on、satisfaction with、pleasure to

聽聽看 6

1. We're going to **listen to** an interview.
2. My **pleasure to** be here.
3. The basic message here is **focusing on** how you sell instead of just **relying on** the product.
4. The customer is **pulling back**.
5. They wanted to **find out** what makes them willing to …
6. Customer loyalty is not necessarily **tied to** just product quality.
7. Customers place significantly greater **emphasis on** their **satisfaction with** the sales experience.
8. They **commit to** a particular supplier.

動動腦 7

1. How do you retain customers through the downturn?
2. Are you emphasizing a focus on service?
3. How do you increase customer retention when the customer is pulling back?
4. What are those strategies?
5. What do you mean by that?
6. What's an overall loyalty index?

CD 內容

Track 15

A：We're going to listen to an interview with Dan Welch, marketing guru, about how to retain customers in these difficult times. Hi Dan, thanks for joining us.

B：You're welcome, my pleasure to be here.

A：So Dan, let me begin with the most crucial matter: how do you retain customers through the downturn?

B：The basic message here is focusing on how you sell instead of just relying on the product or the brand to do your work for you.

A：So are you emphasizing a focus on service?

B：Yes. Service excellence can increase customer retention by up to 20% and shorten the sales cycle by 25%.

A：I see. But how do you increase customer retention when the customer is pulling back?

B：The Corporate Executive Board's Sales and Marketing Practice surveyed more than 5,000 individuals at its members' customer organizations. They wanted to find out what makes them willing to: 1) keep buying from that supplier, 2) buy even more over time, and 3) promote that supplier's reputation to their own business contacts. The results reveal clear but unexpected strategies for winning that kind of loyalty in a down economy.

A：Oh I see, and what are those strategies?

B：Well, there are basically three. First. It's not what you sell but how you sell it.

A：Oh, really? What do you mean by that?

B： Contrary to conventional wisdom, customer loyalty is not necessarily tied to just product quality, brand recognition, and service excellence. While those things matter, customers place significantly greater emphasis on their satisfaction with the sales experience itself when they commit to a particular supplier. This accounts for 53% of a customer's overall loyalty index.

A： What's an overall loyalty index?

B： A loyalty index is a marketing tool we use to discover and measure the different factors which create loyalty for a customer ...

【中譯】

A：我們即將收聽一段與行銷大師 Dan Welch 的訪談，談談在這麼艱困的時期要如何留住顧客。嗨，Dan，謝謝你到節目來。

B：不客氣，我很榮幸來上節目。

A：那麼，Dan，我就從最重要的議題開始：你在經濟衰退時期要如何留住顧客呢？

B：最基本的要點著眼於你如何銷售，而不是只靠產品或是品牌來幫你做銷售。

A：所以你是強調要著重服務嗎？

B：是的。優質服務可以提高 20% 的客戶維繫，並縮短 25% 的銷售週期。

A：我懂了。可是當客戶在縮減消費的時候，你要如何提高客戶維繫呢？

B：企業執行委員會的市場行銷單位針對會員的客戶組織做了超過 5 千人的調查，希望找出為何他們願意：1) 持續向該家供應商購買、2) 隨著時間愈買愈多，和 3) 把該家供應商的聲譽宣傳給與自己有業務往來的客戶。結果顯示，在經濟蕭條時期要贏得忠誠度的策略很顯而易見，但也很出人意外。

A：喔，這樣啊，那是哪些策略呢？

B：嗯，基本上有三個。首先，重點不是你銷售什麼而是你如何銷售。

A：噢，真的嗎？這是什麼意思呢？

B：不同於一般認知，顧客忠誠度不見得只和產品品質、品牌知名度和優質服務有關。這些事情當然也重要，但客戶更注重的是，在和特定一家供應商合作時對於銷售體驗本身的滿意度。這一點占了顧客整體忠誠度指數的 53% 。

A：什麼是整體忠誠度指數？

B：忠誠度指數是一種行銷工具，我們用來發現和評量引發客戶對品牌忠誠的各種因素……

Unit 7

Barnes and Noble

美國書商 Barnes and Noble

學習重點 公司介紹、行銷策略

聽聽看

1 請聽一段美國書商 Barnes and Noble 的介紹，你可以聽懂多少呢？在聽之前，請看看下列字彙，你覺得哪些字會出現在這段聽力中呢。 Track 17

- ☐ audio 聲音的
- ☐ book 書
- ☐ marketing 行銷
- ☐ picture 照片
- ☐ video 影像
- ☐ author 作者
- ☐ coffeehouse 咖啡館
- ☐ paper 紙
- ☐ retail 零售
- ☐ writer 寫者

小叮嚀

藉由這些單字提示，對你聽懂這段公司介紹是否有幫助呢？請在下列線段標示出你的理解程度，在本章最後，我們會再次做相同的評量，看看你進步了多少。

0%　10%　20%　30%　40%　50%　60%　70%　80%　90%　100%

聽聽看

2 請再聽一次 Barnes and Noble 的介紹，以下陳述如果「正確」，請標示 T；「錯誤」者請標示 F。 Track 17

例	Barnes & Noble 是美國最大書商。	T
1	它擁有超過 1 萬家書店。	
2	書店數量每個月都在增加。	
3	公司也擁有小型連鎖書店。	
4	公司只銷售書籍。	
5	他們是美國最大的咖啡館。	

6	他們把最現代的行銷技術引進圖書銷售。	
7	他們只銷售暢銷書。	
8	他們銷售的書籍種類很少。	
9	他們經營的是道德事業。	

答案 請見71頁。

如果聽第一次時無法完全掌握上述訊息，請多練習幾次。接著，我們來學習介紹公司和談論行銷時會用到的字彙。

動動腦 3 連連看，請將下列字彙與正確意思配對。見範例。

■ top bookseller brand •	• 年度調查
■ diverse titles •	• 唱片精選
■ audio selections •	• 客戶服務訂單
■ innovative marketing techniques •	• 廣泛的書目
■ mail order •	• 道德事業經營
■ online ordering •	• 愈來愈高的百分比
■ customer service orders •	• 創新的行銷技術
■ small publishers •	• 郵購
■ university presses •	• 線上訂購
■ growing percentage •	• 小型出版社
■ vast selection •	• 頂尖的書商品牌
■ ethical business practices •	• 最高評比
■ top rating •	• 大學出版協會
■ annual survey •	• 大量的選擇

答案 請見 71 頁。核對完答案，請花點時間熟悉這些字彙，並跟著 CD 練習發音。 Track 18

請再回頭聽一次公司介紹，並留意上列字彙在上下文的使用方式，如有需要可以參閱本章末的 CD 內容，將聽力段落當成字彙的使用範文來學習。

在介紹公司時，不免需要提及數據資訊，我們接著來練習這些數字。

說說看

4 請跟著 CD 練習下列數字的發音。 Track 19

- 1,000
- 8 million
- 50,000
- 300 million
- 4,000
- 100 percent
- 49
- 5%

在這段公司介紹中，出現了二個片語 account for 和 make up，你有察覺到嗎？它們的意思是相同的喔。

動動腦

5 account for 和 make up 的意思為何？請勾選最貼切的解釋。

account for sth. = make up sth.	
	form part of and be the reason for something
	count something
	do accounting

答案 如果摸不著頭緒，可以藉由聽力段落的上下文，判斷它們所指為何。答案請見 72 頁。

同本書先前所提，公司介紹大部分是在陳述事實，所以動詞使用現在簡單式。

動動腦 **4** 請以下列單字填空完成句子，有些動詞可重複使用。

be committed to	**sell**
reach	**be famous for**
attract	**earn**
have	**take**
be administered by	**make up**

1. Barnes & Noble ________ over 1,000 bookstores.

2. It ________ just over 300 million books.

3. Its chain of stores ________ 49 states.

4. Diverse titles ________ many customers.

5. The company ________ introducing innovative marketing techniques.

6. The company ________ more than 8 million customer service orders.

7. Small publishers and university presses ________ a growing percentage of their business.

8. They ________ carrying a vast selection of titles.

9. Barnes & Noble regularly ________ the top rating of 100 percent.

10. An annual survey which ________ the Human Rights Campaign Foundation.

答案 請見72頁。請留意主詞和動詞的一致性。

說說看

7 請使用你在本章學會的用語，為這段公司介紹做個摘要，並練習開口說。

小叮嚀

請把你的口說摘要錄音，並聽錄音評量自己的進步狀況。可以多練習幾次，直到可以說得流利。

聽聽看

8 最後請再聽一次公司介紹，並在下列線段標示出你的理解程度。經過一連串學習，你的聽力理解進步了嗎？如果沒有，請再回頭針對弱項加強。 Track 17

0%　10%　20%　30%　40%　50%　60%　70%　80%　90%　100%

解答

聽聽看 2

1. F，它擁有超過 1 千家。
2. T
3. T
4. F，他們也銷售影片和唱片專輯。
5. F，是第二大。
6. T
7. F，他們也銷售小型出版社和大學出版協會的書籍。
8. F，他們的書籍種類很廣泛。
9. T

動動腦 3

top bookseller brand	頂尖的書商品牌
diverse titles	廣泛的書目
audio selections	唱片精選
innovative marketing techniques	創新的行銷技術
mail order	郵購
online ordering	線上訂購
customer service orders	客戶服務訂單
small publishers	小型出版社
university presses	大學出版協會
growing percentage	愈來愈高的百分比
vast selection	大量的選擇
ethical business practices	道德事業經營
top rating	最高評比
annual survey	年度調查

動動腦 5

account for sth. = make up sth.

= **form part of and be the reason for something** 占；說明……的原因

動動腦 6

1. Barnes & Noble **has** over 1,000 bookstores.
2. It **sells** just over 300 million books.
3. Its chain of stores **reaches** 49 states.
4. Diverse titles **attract** many customers.
5. The company **is famous for** introducing innovative marketing techniques.
6. The company **takes** more than 8 million customer service orders.
7. Small publishers and university presses **make up** a growing percentage of their business.
8. They **are committed to** carrying a vast selection of titles.
9. Barnes & Noble regularly **earns** the top rating of 100 percent.
10. An annual survey which **is administered by** the Human Rights Campaign Foundation.

CD 內容

Track 17

Barnes & Noble is the largest bookseller in the United States and the nation's top bookseller brand. It has over 1,000 bookstores and sells just over 300 million books a year. Its chain of stores reaches 49 states, and the number of stores increases monthly. The superstores, such as the famous Barnes and Noble in New York, are a big success, but the smaller bookstores such as B. Dalton Booksellers lose profit. The superstores have more than hundreds of thousands of diverse titles that attract many customers. They also have small restaurants, entertainment, and newer video and audio selections. They are the second largest coffee house in the United States.

The company is famous for introducing innovative marketing techniques, such as mail order and online ordering, into the world of bookselling. The company takes more than 8 million customer service orders in one year, and 4,000 in one day. Bestsellers account for less than 5% of their sales, and more than 50,000 small publishers and university presses make up a growing percentage of their business. They are committed to carrying a vast selection of titles from many publishers, large and small. In terms of ethical business practices, Barnes & Noble regularly earns the top rating of 100 percent in the Corporate Equality Index, an annual survey which is administered by the Human Rights Campaign Foundation.

【中譯】

Barnes & Noble 是美國最大書商和全國頂尖的書商品牌，擁有超過 1 千家書店，一年賣出超過 3 億冊書籍。連鎖書店遍及 49 個州，書店數量每個月都在增加。像知名的紐約 Barnes and Noble 等超級書店大獲成功，但 B. Dalton Booksellers 等小型書店卻出現虧損。超級書店內擁有數十萬冊各類書籍，吸引了許多顧客，店內還有小餐廳、娛樂場所，和較新的影片和唱片可供選擇，是美國的第二大咖啡館。

該公司以把創新行銷技術引進圖書銷售業界而聞名，例如郵購和線上訂購。公司一年接到的客戶服務訂單有 800 萬筆以上，一天超過 4 千筆。暢銷書占不到業績的 5%，但是超過 5 萬家的小出版社和大學出版協會則占了業績愈來愈大的百分比。他們致力於經銷許多大大小小出版社的大量書籍。在道德商業經營方面，Barnes & Noble 在人權運動基金會進行的「企業平等指數」年度調查中，經常贏得 100% 的最高評比。

Unit 8

Visa Fraud
簽證詐欺

學習重點 外籍勞動市場（英國口音）

聽聽看

1 請聽一段關於美國簽證詐欺的報導，你可以聽懂多少呢？在聽之前，請看看下列字彙，你覺得哪些字會出現在這段聽力中呢。 Track 20

- ☐ abuse 濫用
- ☐ arrest 逮捕
- ☐ bank 銀行
- ☐ credit card 信用卡
- ☐ debt 負債
- ☐ fraud 詐欺
- ☐ loan 貸款
- ☐ plastic 塑膠的；人工的
- ☐ unemployment 失業
- ☐ worker 工人

小叮嚀

藉由這些單字提示，對你聽懂這段報導是否有幫助呢？請在下列線段標示出你的理解程度，在本章最後，我們會再次做相同的評量，看看你進步了多少。

0% 10% 20% 30% 40% 50% 60% 70% 80% 90% 100%

聽聽看

2 請再聽一次報導，以下陳述如果「正確」，請標示 T；「錯誤」者請標示 F。 Track 20

例	電腦科技產業的簽證詐欺事件頗有爭議。	T
1	H-1B 簽證方案是針對低技能勞工的。	
2	在 11 個州有 6 個人遭到逮捕。	
3	防止簽證詐欺事件已經進行 18 個月。	
4	H-1B 簽證系統不是第一次遭到調查了。	
5	此系統被批評將廉價的科技勞工引進美國。	

6	這些廉價勞工沒有搶走本國勞工的工作。	
7	Oracle 和 Microsoft 希望降低雇用外國勞工的限額。	
8	Microsoft 和政府一起為此議題而努力。	

答案 請見 81 頁。

如果聽第一次時無法完全掌握上述訊息，請多練習幾次。接著，我們來學習談論勞動市場時會用到的字彙。

動動腦 3 連連看，請將下列字彙與正確意思配對。見範例。

■ nationwide controversy •	• 處理問題
■ visa program •	• 招致批評
■ highly skilled workers •	• 犯下詐欺罪
■ federal agents •	• （法律）執行上的努力
■ wide investigation •	• 聯邦幹員
■ suspected visa fraud •	• 偽造……的身份
■ fraudulently represent sb. •	• 高技能勞工
■ immigration documents •	• 移民文件
■ enforcement effort •	• 全國性的爭議
■ address the problem •	• 潛在的影響
■ attract criticism •	• 提高每年限額
■ potential effects •	• 疑似簽證詐欺
■ raise the annual limit •	• 簽證方案
■ commit fraud •	• 全面的調查

答案 請見 81 頁。核對完答案，請花點時間熟悉這些字彙，並跟著 CD 練習發音。 Track 21

請再回頭聽一次報導，並留意上列字彙在上下文的使用方式，如有需要可以參閱本章末的CD內容，將聽力段落當成字彙的使用範文來學習。

動動腦

4 在報導中，heating up 一詞被用來描述爭議，請勾選它的正確意思。

	a controversy is heating up
	it's getting more difficult to get people interested in the issue
	an argument or debate is getting worse
	the weather is getting hot

答案 如果摸不著頭緒，可以藉由聽力段落的上下文，判斷此用語所指為何。答案請見82頁。

說說看

5 請研讀下列談論犯罪時常用的字串，請跟著CD練習發音。 Track 22

- detain sb. 扣留某人
- an investigation into sth. 針對某事進行的調查
- suspected fraud 疑似詐欺
- be arrested 遭到逮捕
- be accused of 被指控……
- do sth. fraudulently 以詐欺手段做某事

聽聽看

6 請再聽一次報導，並以上一題的字串完成這些句子。 Track 20

1. Federal agents have ____________ 11 people.

2. … a wide ____________ into ____________ visa ____________.

3. Those who have been ____________ are ____________ of ____________ representing themselves.

答案 請見 82 頁。

我們在 Unit 3 學過一些談論目前趨勢和當前狀態的動詞，而這一段報導也是屬於目前狀況的描述。

動動腦 7 如果要將下列字串分成三類，你會怎麼分呢？

- have been arrested 被逮捕
- have detained 拘留
- has been operating 一直被操作
- has been working 一直在工作
- are seeking to 正在尋求
- is rising 正在升高
- are using 正在使用
- is heating up 愈演愈烈
- is coming under fire 被批評
- is continuing 正在繼續

答案 請見 82 頁。希望你可以看出它們可分為：have + p.p. 動詞字串、be Ving 動詞字串、have been Ving 動詞字串。

分析

- 這些動詞字串都可用來描述一個目前的情況。
- have + p.p. 字串著重於現在的結果；be Ving 和 have been Ving 字串則著重於目前的活動、或是目前的趨勢，無關乎結果。

聽聽看

8 請再聽一次報導，並以上一題的字串完成這些句子。

Track 20

1. The nationwide controversy is ____________ once again.
2. The coordinated enforcement effort ____________ for 18 months.
3. The effort ____________.
4. Unemployment ____________ in the U.S.
5. The H-1B program ____________.
6. Some IT firms ____________ H-1B visas.
7. Oracle and Microsoft ____________ to differentiate themselves.
8. The company ____________ with the government.

答案 請見 82 頁。

說說看

9 請使用你在本章學會的用語，為這段報導做個摘要，並練習開口說。

小叮嚀

請把你的口說摘要錄音，並聽錄音評量自己的進步狀況。可以多練習幾次，直到可以說得流利。

聽聽看

10 最後請再聽一次報導，並在下列線段標示出你的理解程度。經過一連串學習，你的聽力理解進步了嗎？如果沒有，請再回頭針對弱項加強。 Track 20

0% — 10% — 20% — 30% — 40% — 50% — 60% — 70% — 80% — 90% — 100%

解答

聽聽看 2

1. F，是針對高技能勞工的。
2. F，在 6 個州 11 個人遭到逮捕。
3. T
4. F，這是第一次。
5. T
6. F，他們搶走了本國勞工的工作。
7. F，他們希望提高限額。
8. T

動動腦 3

nationwide controversy	全國性的爭議
visa program	簽證方案
highly skilled workers	高技能勞工
federal agents	聯邦幹員
wide investigation	全面的調查
suspected visa fraud	疑似簽證詐欺
fraudulently represent sb.	偽造……的身份
immigration documents	移民文件
enforcement effort	（法律）執行上的努力
address the problem	處理問題
attract criticism	招致批評
potential effects	潛在的影響
raise the annual limit	提高每年限額
commit fraud	犯下詐欺罪

動動腦 4

a controversy is heating up

= **an argument or debate is getting worse** 爭議愈演愈烈

聽聽看 6

1. Federal agents have **detained** 11 people.
2. ... a wide **investigation** into **suspected** visa **fraud**.
3. Those who have been **arrested** are **accused** of **fraudulently** representing themselves.

動動腦 7

可分為三類：

have + p.p. 動詞字串： have been arrested 、 have detained

be Ving 動詞字串：is rising 、 are using 、 is heating up 、 is coming under fire 、 are seeking to 、 is continuing

have been Ving 動詞字串： has been operating 、 has been working

聽聽看 8

1. The nationwide controversy **is heating up** once again.
2. The coordinated enforcement effort **has been operating** for 18 months.
3. The effort **is continuing**.
4. Unemployment **is rising** in the U.S.
5. The H-1B program **is coming under fire**.
6. Some IT firms **are using** H-1B visas.
7. Oracle and Microsoft **are seeking** to differentiate themselves.
8. The company **has been working** with the government.

CD 內容

Track 20

The nationwide controversy over the H-1B visa program for highly skilled workers is heating up once again. Federal agents have detained 11 people in six states as part of a wide investigation into suspected visa fraud. Those who have been arrested are accused of fraudulently representing themselves or other workers in immigration documents.

The coordinated enforcement effort has been operating for 18 months and the effort is continuing, officials said. It is the first to specifically address the problem of fraud in the H-1B visa system, which critics say brings lower-cost tech workers into the U.S., displacing American workers.

As unemployment is rising in the U.S., the H-1B program is coming under fire for its potential effects on U.S. jobs. Critics say that some IT firms, including Infosys Technologies and Wipro, are using H-1B visas to replace U.S. employees with cheaper workers from abroad.

However, other large U.S. tech companies such as Oracle and Microsoft, which want to raise the annual limits on H-1B visas, are seeking to differentiate themselves from firms that commit fraud. Bill Kamela, director of policy counsel for Microsoft, told reporters in January that the company has been working with the government to ensure the program is free from fraud.

【中譯】

全國對於高技能勞工 H-1B 簽證方案（譯註）的爭議又再一次升溫。在全面調查疑似簽證詐欺案件的過程，聯邦幹員在六個州拘留了 11 個人，遭逮捕者被指控在移民文件中偽造個人或其他勞工的身份。

官方表示採取聯合執法的努力已進行 18 個月，而且仍在繼續。批評人士認為 H-1B 簽證系統引進廉價科技勞工到美國並取代了美國本土勞工，這是首次專門處理 H-1B 系統的詐欺問題。

失業率在美國日益上升，H-1B 方案因為對美國工作的潛在影響而遭受抨擊。批評人士說某些資訊科技公司，包括 Infosys Technologies 和 Wipro 都使用 H-1B 簽證，以外來較低價的勞工取代美國員工。

不過，其他像 Oracle 和 Microsoft 等希望提高 H-1B 簽證每年限額的美國大型科技公司，則想辦法要和犯下詐欺情事的公司做切割。 Microsoft 的政策顧問主任 Bill Kamela 在一月份時告訴記者，他們公司一直與政府共同努力，確保這項方案沒有詐欺之虞。

〔譯註〕H-1B visa 爲短期受雇美國公司的特殊專業外籍人士工作簽證，必須由美國雇主提出申請，每年的常規名額爲 65,000 名，碩士以上高學歷名額爲 20,000 名，移民局 4 月 1 日開始接受申請，經常第一天就額滿。多位國會議員曾經提出議案，要求增加每年的名額，以適應美國高科技公司發展的需要。

Unit 9

IT Sector Q1 Results

IT 產業的第一季成果

學習重點 財務報告

聽聽看

1 請聽一段 IT 產業的第一季財務報告，你可以聽懂多少呢？在聽之前，請看看下列字彙，你覺得哪些字會出現在這段聽力中呢。 Track 23

- ☐ California 加州
- ☐ chip 晶片
- ☐ computer 電腦
- ☐ earnings 盈餘
- ☐ history 歷史
- ☐ industry 產業
- ☐ service 服務
- ☐ software 軟體
- ☐ study 學習
- ☐ weather 天氣

小叮嚀

藉由這些單字提示，對你聽懂這段報告是否有幫助呢？請在下列線段標示出你的理解程度，在本章最後，我們會再次做相同的評量，看看你進步了多少。

0% — 10% — 20% — 30% — 40% — 50% — 60% — 70% — 80% — 90% — 100%

聽聽看

2 請再聽一次報告，以下陳述如果「正確」，請標示 T；「錯誤」者請標示 F。 Track 23

例	報告是關於電腦科技公司的第一季成果。	T
1	HP 獲利減少是因為營收減少。	
2	HP 調降了它的年度獲利預測。	
3	HP 的股票在新聞報導之後下跌。	
4	HP 一直沒辦法減少開支。	
5	HP 在這場經濟危機中表現的比其他電腦科技公司差。	

6	其他公司的第一季成果都沒有不好。	
7	Microsoft 宣布裁員。	
8	Cisco Systems 公布訂單增加。	

答案 請見 91 頁。

如果聽第一次時無法完全掌握上述訊息，請多練習幾次。接著，我們來學習談論財務狀況時會用到的字彙。

動動腦 **3** 連連看，請將下列字彙與正確意思配對。

personal computer	盤後交易
first-quarter earnings	多樣的產品項目
quick rebound	競爭激烈的市場
full-year earnings	削減成本的努力
net income	工廠生產力
after-hours trading	第一季獲利
market close	全年度獲利
broad portfolio	全球經濟衰退
cost-cutting efforts	股市收盤
global economic downturn	淨所得
challenging market	個人電腦
tech companies	迅速回升
factory capacity	緩慢成長
slow growth	科技公司

答案 請見 91 頁。核對完答案，請花點時間熟悉這些字彙，並跟著 CD 練習發音。 Track 24

請再回頭聽一次報導，並留意上列字彙在上下文的使用方式，如有需要可以參閱本章末的CD內容，將聽力段落當成字彙的使用範文來學習。

數據資訊是財務報告中的固定班底，我們就不厭其煩地再來熟悉它們的唸法吧。

說說看 4 請跟著CD練習這些數字和日期的發音。 Track 25

- April 3rd
- March 31st
- $2.1 billion
- $28.4 billion
- 32.9
- 13%
- $1.9 billion
- 80¢
- 93¢
- 1%
- 79¢
- $28.8 billion
- 6%

在這段財務報告中，出現了weather這個字。Weather當名詞用時，為「天氣」之意，但此處weather被當成動詞來使用，你能看出它的意思為何嗎？

動動腦 5 Weather這個動詞的意思為何？請勾選最貼切的解釋。

weather sth.	
	have bad weather
	be ill
	survive a difficult situation

答案 如果摸不著頭緒，可以藉由聽力段落的上下文，判斷它的意思為何。答案請見92頁。

動動腦 6 如果要將下列字串分成二類，你會怎麼分呢？

- be no quick recovery 沒有迅速回升
- reported slow growth 報告成長緩慢
- saw an increase 看見增加
- was a slight rise 略微上升
- declined 下降
- retreated 撤退
- tumbled 突然下跌
- weakened 變弱

答案 請見 92 頁。核對完答案，請跟著 CD 練習這些字串的發音。

Track 26

聽聽看 7 請再聽一次報告，並以上一題的字串完成這些句子。

Track 23

1. Hewlett-Packard on April 3rd reported that first-quarter earnings ____________ 13%.
2. There was ____________ in revenue of 1%.
3. There would ____________.
4. Revenue ____________ to $28.8 billion.
5. HP's stock ____________ in after-hours trading.
6. Sales of personal computers ____________ sharply.
7. Cisco Systems ____________.
8. Orders for its products ____________ markedly.

答案 請見 92 頁。

說說看

8 請使用你在本章學會的用語，為這段報告做個摘要，並練習開口說。

小叮嚀

請把你的口說摘要錄音，並聽錄音評量自己的進步狀況。可以多練習幾次，直到可以說得流利。

聽聽看

9 最後請再聽一次報告，並在下列線段標示出你的理解程度。經過一連串學習，你的聽力理解進步了嗎？如果沒有，請再回頭針對弱項加強。 Track 23

○	○	○	○	○	○	○	○	○	○	○
0%	10%	20%	30%	40%	50%	60%	70%	80%	90%	100%

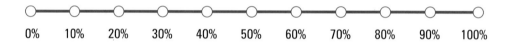

解答

聽聽看 2

1. F，營收增加了一點點。
2. T
3. T
4. F，公司已經削減支出。
5. F，表現的比其他公司好。
6. F，他們的第一季成果全都欠佳。
7. T
8. F，訂單減少。

動動腦 3

personal computer	個人電腦
first-quarter earnings	第一季獲利
quick rebound	迅速回升
full-year earnings	全年度獲利
net income	淨所得
after-hours trading	盤後交易
market close	股市收盤
broad portfolio	多樣的產品項目
cost-cutting efforts	削減成本的努力
global economic downturn	全球經濟衰退
challenging market	競爭激烈的市場
tech companies	科技公司
factory capacity	工廠生產力
slow growth	緩慢成長

動動腦 5

weather sth. = **survive a difficult situation** 安然度過艱困時期

動動腦 6

這些字串大都表示負面意思，除了 **was a slight rise** 和 **saw an increase** 有表示正面、向上提升的意思。

聽聽看 7

1. Hewlett-Packard on April 3rd reported that first-quarter earnings **tumbled** 13%.
2. There **was a slight rise** in revenue of 1%.
3. There would **be no quick recovery**.
4. Revenue **saw an increase** to $28.8 billion.
5. HP's stock **retreated** in after-hours trading.
6. Sales of personal computers **weakened** sharply.
7. Cisco Systems **reported slow growth**.
8. Orders for its products **declined** markedly.

CD 內容

Track 23

Amid a broad-based decline in its core personal computer and printer businesses, Hewlett-Packard on April 3rd reported that first-quarter earnings tumbled 13%, despite the fact that there was a slight rise in revenue of 1%. The company predicted that there would be no quick recovery in its fortunes and cut its full-year earnings forecast.

HP, which makes computers, printers, software, and other products, reported that net income for the three months ended on March 31st fell to $1.9 billion, or 79¢ a share, from $2.1 billion, or 80¢ a share a year ago. Revenue saw an increase to $28.8 billion from $28.4 billion.

The company met Wall Street expectations that it would earn 93¢ a share. HP's stock retreated in after-hours trading. It was down about 6% from the market close to 32.9 a share.

Despite the weaker performance, the technology giant's broad portfolio of products and services and intense cost-cutting efforts appear to be helping it weather the global economic downturn better than most of its peers. "HP performed well in a challenging market," said Mark Hurd, HP chairman and chief executive officer.

Other tech companies also had a bad time in Quarter 1. Chipmakers Intel and Advanced Micro Devices cut costs and reduced factory capacity as sales of personal computers weakened sharply. Microsoft, meanwhile, announced the first layoffs in its history, and Cisco Systems reported slow growth as orders for its products declined markedly. PC maker Dell reports its earnings next week.

【中譯】

在核心產品個人電腦與印表機業績持續下滑之際，Hewlett-Packard（HP）四月三日公布第一季獲利狂跌 13%，但事實上營收小幅增加 1%。該公司預言下滑情形不會迅速回升，並調降了全年度的獲利預測。

生產電腦、印表機、軟體與其他產品的 HP 公布結算至三月 31 日的三個月淨所得減少為 19 億美元，每股 0.79 美元，去年同期為 21 億美元，每股 0.80 美元。營收則是從 284 億美元增加為 288 億美元

公司股價符合華爾街預期，每股盈利為 0.93 美元。 HP 股票的盤後交易下挫，比起收盤時下跌了 6%，來到每股 32.9 美元。

儘管表現不若以往強勁，這家科技巨人的多樣化產品、服務和密集削減成本的努力，似乎幫助了它比起大多數同業更安然度過這場全球性的經濟衰退風暴。 HP 的主席暨執行長 Mark Hurd 表示：「HP 在充滿挑戰的市場上表現良好。」

其他科技公司在第一季也很難熬。由於個人電腦的銷售量大幅衰減，晶片製造廠 Intel 和 Advanced Micro Devices 減少開支並降低工廠生產量。在此同時，Microsoft 也宣布了公司成立以來的首次裁員，Cisco System 也公布由於產品訂單明顯減少而使業績成長減緩。個人電腦製造廠 Dell 會在下週公布公司營收。

Unit 10

The World's Back Office

世界的後端辦公室

學習重點 委外代工（英國口音）

聽聽看

1 請聽一段關於美國外包政策的報導，你可以聽懂多少呢？在聽之前，請看看下列字彙，你覺得哪些字會出現在這段聽力中呢。 Track 27

- ☐ complain 抱怨
- ☐ economy 經濟
- ☐ international 國際的
- ☐ outsourcing 外包
- ☐ sea 海
- ☐ ship 用船載運
- ☐ speech 演說
- ☐ tax 稅
- ☐ tomorrow 明天
- ☐ transport 運輸

小叮嚀

藉由這些單字提示，對你聽懂這段報導是否有幫助呢？請在下列線段標示出你的理解程度，在本章最後，我們會再次做相同的評量，看看你進步了多少。

○—○—○—○—○—○—○—○—○—○—○

0% 10% 20% 30% 40% 50% 60% 70% 80% 90% 100%

聽聽看

2 請再聽一次報導，以下陳述如果「正確」，請標示 **T**；「錯誤」者請標示 **F**。 Track 27

例	印度民衆擔心美國將會改變外包政策。	T
1	外包服務是印度經濟成長最快的產業之一。	
2	美國總統的新預算將使把工作外包至海外的公司更容易獲得減稅。	
3	印度的資訊科技產業占了全國國民生產毛額的 7%。	
4	印度的經濟正在衰退。	
5	印度政府並不反對貿易保護主義。	

6	印度政府擔心這項政策的改變。	
7	每個人都知道美國政府接下來會怎麼做。	

答案 請見 101 頁。

如果聽第一次時無法完全掌握上述訊息，請多練習幾次。接著，我們來學習談論外包政策時會用到的字彙。

動動腦 **3** 連連看，請將下列字彙與正確意思配對。

back office	後端辦公室
slowdown	杜絕；消弭
ship jobs overseas	政府官員
tax benefits	誘因；動機
government officials	缺乏明確性
slowing economy	反對貿易保護主義
tax cuts	外包產業
spending plans	將工作外包至海外
opposing protectionism	衰退
outsourcing industry	不振的經濟
lack of clarity	消費方案
eliminate	稅務福利
incentives	減稅

答案 請見 101 頁。核對完答案，請花點時間熟悉這些字彙，並跟著 CD 練習發音。 Track 28

請再回頭聽一次報導，並留意上列字彙在上下文的使用方式，如有需要可以參閱本章末的 CD 內容，將聽力段落當成字彙的使用範文來學習。

這段報導中使用了幾個俚語，我們接著來學習它們的用法。

動動腦 4 請勾選最貼切的解釋。

	cast a shadow over sth.
	put something in the dark
	have a negative impact on sth.

	be vexing
	be worrying
	be trying

	have a stake in sth.
	eat beef
	have an investment in sth.

答案 如果摸不著頭緒，可以藉由聽力段落的上下文，判斷它們的意思為何。答案請見 102 頁。

報導中所談及的潛在政策改變，所造成的影響會在未來發生。所以報導中用了許多表達未來的字串，有一些是確定的未來，有一些則是不確定的未來。

動動腦 **5** 請將下列未來字串分類並填入下表。

- will V
- are likely to V
- is planning to V
- might be coming next
- is not providing
- could V
- may V
- will have to V
- intend to V
- is thinking of Ving
- are going to have to V

確定	不確定

答案 請見 102 頁。核對完答案，請跟著 CD 練習這些字串的發音。

Track 29

聽聽看 **6** 請再聽一次報導，並以上一題的字串完成這些句子。

Track 27

1. The new President's policies ________ cast a shadow over one of the fastest-growing sectors of their economy.
2. The budget the President recently presented ________ make it harder for U.S. companies.
3. The moves ________ worry government officials.

4. We __________ address this issue.

5. The government __________ launch tax cuts.

6. We __________ oppose protectionism.

7. There is a lack of clarity about what __________ from the U.S.

8. The administration __________ eliminating incentives.

9. The White House __________ additional details.

10. Indians with a stake in the outsourcing industry __________ wait and watch.

11. Nobody knows what they __________ do next.

答案 請見 102 頁。

說說看

7 請使用你在本章學會的用語，為這段報導做個摘要，並練習開口說。

小叮嚀

請把你的口說摘要錄音，並聽錄音評量自己的進步狀況。可以多練習幾次，直到可以說得流利。

聽聽看

8 最後請再聽一次報導，並在下列線段標示出你的理解程度。經過一連串學習，你的聽力理解進步了嗎？如果沒有，請再回頭針對弱項加強。 Track 27

0% — 10% — 20% — 30% — 40% — 50% — 60% — 70% — 80% — 90% — 100%

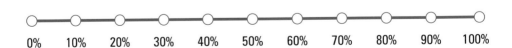

解答

聽聽看 2

1. T
2. F，會使他們更難獲得。
3. T
4. T
5. F，他們反對。
6. T
7. F，沒有人知道。

動動腦 3

back office	後端辦公室
slowdown	衰退
ship jobs overseas	將工作外包至海外
tax benefits	稅務福利
government officials	政府官員
slowing economy	不振的經濟
tax cuts	減稅
spending plans	消費方案
opposing protectionism	反對貿易保護主義
outsourcing industry	外包產業
lack of clarity	缺乏明確性
eliminate	杜絕；消弭
incentives	誘因；動機

動動腦 4

- cast a shadow over sth.
  = **have a negative impact on sth.** 對……有負面影響
- be vexing = **be worrying** 擔心
- have a stake in sth. = **have an investment in sth.** 投資……

動動腦 5

確定	不確定
• intend to V • is not providing • are going to have to V • will V • will have to V • is planning to V	• might be coming next • is thinking of Ving • could V • may V • are likely to V

聽聽看 6

1. The new President's policies **will** cast a shadow over one of the fastest-growing sectors of their economy.
2. The budget the President recently presented **may** make it harder for U.S. companies.
3. The moves **are likely to** worry government officials.
4. We **will have to** address this issue.
5. The government **is planning to** launch tax cuts.
6. We **intend to** oppose protectionism.
7. There is a lack of clarity about what **might be coming next** from the U.S.
8. The administration **is thinking of** eliminating incentives.
9. The White House **is not providing** additional details.
10. Indians with a stake in the outsourcing industry **are going to have to** wait and watch.
11. Nobody knows what they **could** do next.

CD 內容

Track 27

After a decade of outsourcing helped transform India into much of the world's back office, Indians are worried that President Obama's new administration — and the slowdown in the global economy — will cast a shadow over one of the fastest-growing sectors of their economy. The budget the President recently presented may make it harder for U.S. companies that send jobs overseas to receive tax benefits.

In India, where the $63 billion IT sector makes up almost 7% of the national GDP, the moves are likely to worry government officials. Pranab Mukherjee, a minor government official, was already complaining about it over the weekend. "We will have to address this issue," said Mukherjee. The government is planning to launch tax cuts and spending plans to try to revive India's slowing economy. "We intend to oppose protectionism, not only here but at every forum."

Even more vexing for India's outsourcing industry is the fact that there is a lack of clarity about what might be coming next from the U.S. During a February 24th speech to Congress, Obama said the administration is thinking of eliminating incentives for companies that ship jobs overseas, but the White House is not providing additional details until later in the month.

Indians with a stake in the outsourcing industry are going to have to wait and watch. "Of course we are concerned," says Mohandas Pai, a board member and director of human resources at Infosys, India's second-largest IT company by revenues, "but nobody knows what they could do next."

【中譯】

經過十年的外包服務讓印度搖身一變成為世界的後端辦公室，而今印度人擔心美國總統歐巴馬的新行政團隊——和全球經濟衰退——將會使他們經濟成長最快的產業之一蒙上陰影。美國總統最近提出的預算可能會讓外包工作到海外的美國公司更難獲得稅務福利。

在印度，630 億美元的資訊科技產業占了全國國民生產毛額將近 7% ，這些舉動很可能要讓政府官員們憂心了。一位低層官員 Pranab Mukherjee 整個週末都在對此表示抗議， Mukherjee 表示：「我們必須著手處理這個問題。」印度政府正計畫推動減稅和消費方案，盡力振興印度不振的經濟。「我們打算反對貿易保護主義，不只是在這裡而是在每一場經濟討論會上。」

讓印度外包產業更困擾的是，事實上他們無法明確知道美國接下來的可能作法。在二月 24 日對國會的演說中，歐巴馬表示政府團隊想消除公司將工作外包至海外的誘因，不過白宮直到二月底前都沒有提出更多細節。

與外包產業有利益關係的印度民眾也只能靜觀其變了。在印度年收益排名第二的電腦資訊公司 Infosys 的董事會成員暨人力部門主任 Mohandas Pai 表示：「我們當然很擔心，但是沒有人知道他們接下來可以怎麼做。」

Unit 11

Interview with Dan Welch — Part 2

Dan Welch 訪談錄：第二部分

學習重點 行銷策略

聽聽看

1 請聽行銷大師 Dan Welch 的訪談後半段。Dan Welch 擁有自己的顧問公司，專門協助企業在經濟衰退中留住顧客。在聽之前，請看看下列字彙，你覺得哪些字會出現在這段聽力中呢。 Track 30

- ☐ advertising 廣告
- ☐ advice 建議
- ☐ bill 帳單
- ☐ consultant 顧問
- ☐ counter 櫃台
- ☐ insight 洞察
- ☐ succeed 成功
- ☐ supplier 供應商
- ☐ support 支持
- ☐ wrapping 包裝

小叮嚀

藉由這些單字提示，對你聽懂這段訪談是否有幫助呢？請在下列線段標示出你的理解程度，在本章最後，我們會再次做相同的評量，看看你進步了多少。

○—○—○—○—○—○—○—○—○—○—○

0% 10% 20% 30% 40% 50% 60% 70% 80% 90% 100%

聽聽看

2 請再聽一次訪談，以下陳述如果「正確」，請標示 **T**；「錯誤」者請標示 **F**。 Track 30

例	有三個贏得和留住顧客的策略。	T
1	第二個策略為：把洞察跟顧客分享。	
2	客戶不喜歡會分享如何成功的供應商。	
3	良好服務的一部分是教育和協助客戶。	
4	如果你的客戶倒閉，對你來說是有利的。	
5	第三個策略是：忽略擁護者。	

6	擁護者就是願意為你宣傳口碑的客戶。	
7	決策者會選擇每個團隊成員都喜歡的供應商。	
8	只跟決策者建立關係是很重要的。	

答案 請見 111 頁。

如果聽第一次時無法完全掌握上述訊息，請多練習幾次。接著，我們來學習談論行銷策略時會用到的字彙。

動動腦 **3** 連連看，請將下列字彙與正確意思配對。見範例。

sharing insights	建立關係
higher value	事業夥伴
reduce operating expenses	更高的價值
penetrate new markets	忽略擁護者
reduce risk	開發新市場
ignore advocates	採購決策
word of mouth advertising	降低營運開支
business partners	降低風險
senior decision-makers	上級決策者
purchase decision	分享洞察
widespread support	廣泛的支持
build relationships	口碑宣傳

答案 請見 111 頁。核對完答案，請花點時間熟悉這些字彙，並跟著 CD 練習發音。 Track 31

在這段訪談中，Dan Welch 使用了一個俚語 in a nutshell，你知道它是什麼意思嗎？

動動腦 4 請勾選出 in a nutshell 的正確解釋。

	in a nutshell
	some kind of food
	be in a difficult position
	a short summary of sth.

答案 如果摸不著頭緒，可以藉由聽力段落的上下文，判斷它的意思為何。答案請見 111 頁。

現在我們來學習訪談中使用的一些字串。

動動腦 5 如果要將下列字串分二類，你會怎麼分類呢？

- care about sth.
- have sth. to say about sth.
- identify sth.
- talk about sth.
- tell sb. about sth.
- do sth. for sb.
- help sb.
- share sth. with sb.
- teach sb. sth.
- say something about sth.

答案 請見 112 頁。希望你可以看出這些字串是動詞字串。

聽聽看

6 請再聽一次訪談，並以上一題的字串完成這些句子。

Track 30

1. We ________ before ________ the importance ________ service.
2. Can you ________ something ________ the other two?
3. The second strategy is about ________ the customer any insights you might have.
4. Suppliers who ________ them something new.
5. Suppliers who simply ________ the needs.
6. Good service is to educate and ________ the customer.
7. A customer who is willing to ________ word of mouth advertising ________ you.
8. They tell their friends and colleagues ________ you and your service.
9. The number one thing senior decision-makers care ________.
10. Everyone in the company has good things to say ________ a supplier.

答案 請見 112 頁。

動動腦

7 請將下列單字重新排列、組合成訪談中的問句。

1. you two say can about something the other?

____

2. do what mean you?

____

3. that right is?

____

4. third the strategy what's?

____

5. an what's advocate?

____

6. that why important is?

____

答案 請見 112 頁。熟悉發問方式，可以幫助你在對談中主動提問，延續對話的進行。

說說看

8 請使用你在本章學會的用語，為這段行銷策略訪談做個摘要，並練習開口說。

小叮嚀

請把你的口說摘要錄音，並聽錄音評量自己的進步狀況。可以多練習幾次，直到可以說得流利。

聽聽看

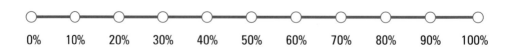

9 最後請再聽一次訪談，並在下列線段標示出你的理解程度。經過一連串學習，你的聽力理解進步了嗎？如果沒有，請再回頭針對弱項加強。 **Track 30**

0% 10% 20% 30% 40% 50% 60% 70% 80% 90% 100%

解答

聽聽看 2

1. T
2. F，他們喜歡把知識跟他們分享的供應商。
3. T
4. F，對你是不利的。
5. F，第三個策略是：不要忽略擁護者。
6. T
7. T
8. F，跟客戶的所有員工、而不只是決策者建立關係是很重要的。

動動腦 3

sharing insights	分享洞察
higher value	更高的價值
reduce operating expenses	降低營運支出
penetrate new markets	開發新市場
reduce risk	降低風險
ignore advocates	忽略擁護者
word of mouth advertising	口碑宣傳
business partners	事業夥伴
senior decision-makers	上級決策者
purchase decision	採購決策
widespread support	廣泛的支持
build relationships	建立關係

動動腦 4

in a nutshell = **a short summary of sth.** 簡單來說；……的簡短摘要

動動腦 5

這些動詞字串可分為二類：

- 含有一個受詞：talk about sth.、identify sth.、help sb.、care about sth.
- 含有兩個受詞：say something about sth.、share sth. with sb.、teach sb. sth.、do sth. for sb.、tell sb. about sth.、have sth. to say about sth.

聽聽看 6

1. We **talked** before **about** the importance of service.
2. Can you **say** something **about** the other two?
3. The second strategy is about **sharing with** the customer any insights you might have.
4. Suppliers who **teach** them something new.
5. Suppliers who simply **identify** the needs.
6. Good service is to educate and **help** the customer.
7. A customer who is willing to **do** word of mouth advertising **for** you.
8. They tell their friends and colleagues **about** you and your service.
9. The number one thing senior decision-makers care **about**.
10. Everyone in the company has good things to say **about** a supplier.

動動腦 7

1. Can you say something about the other two?
2. What do you mean?
3. Is that right?
4. What's the third strategy?
5. What's an advocate?
6. Why is that important?

CD 內容

Track 30

Q：Dan, we talked before about the importance of service in a down market.

A：Yes.

Q：You mentioned in our previous talk that there were three strategies for winning and retaining customers. We already discussed the first one, service. Can you say something about the other two?

A：Yes, indeed. The second strategy is about sharing with the customer any insights you might have.

Q：What do you mean?

A：Within the sales experience, customers place far higher value on suppliers who teach them something new about how to succeed — for example, new ways to reduce operating expenses, penetrate new markets or reduce risk. Alternatively, customers place significantly less value on suppliers who simply identify the needs they already know they have.

Q：Interesting, so you're saying that part of the good service is to educate and help the customer, become more of a partner with them, rather than just simply a supplier. Is that right?

A：Yes, that's right because obviously, if your customer goes out of business, then it's bad for you.

Q：I see, logical. So what's the third strategy?

A：The third strategy is about not ignoring advocates.

Q：What's an advocate?

A：An advocate is a customer who is willing to do word of mouth advertising for you among their own colleagues and business partners, you know, they tell their friends and colleagues about you and your service.

Q：So why is that important?

A：The CEB study found that the number one thing senior decision-makers care about when arriving at a purchase decision is widespread support across their team. If everyone in the company has good things to say about a supplier, then the decision maker will choose that supplier instead of others. On the other hand, if some of the members in the team have bad things to say about the supplier, then the decision maker is more likely to choose another one, one with more support from the entire team.

Q：I see. So it's important to build relationships with all the employees of your customers, not just the decision makers.

A：Yes, in a nutshell.

【中譯】

Q：Dan，我們之前談到服務在市場景氣低迷時的重要性。

A：是的。

Q：在我們上一段談話中，你提到贏得並留住客戶有三個策略。我們已經討論了第一個策略：服務。你可以說說其他兩個策略嗎？

A：當然好。第二個策略是把你可能有的任何洞察跟客戶分享。

Q：這是什麼意思？

A：在銷售體驗當中，客戶對於能教他們新成功方法的供應商會給予更高的評價──例如降低營運支出、開發新市場或降低風險。相反地，對於只是指出已知需求的供應商，客戶給予的評價則要低得多。

Q：很有意思，所以你是說良好服務的其中一部分就是教育和協助客戶，最好能成為他們的夥伴，而不只是一個供應商。這樣說對嗎？

A：是的，這樣說沒錯，因為很顯然的，如果你的客戶倒閉了，那對你來說是不利的。

Q：我懂，這很合邏輯。那第三個策略是什麼？

A：第三個策略是不要忽略擁護者。

Q：何謂擁護者？

A：擁護者就是願意在他們的同事和事業夥伴之間為你做口碑宣傳的客戶，你知道，他們會跟朋友和同事談起你和你的服務。

Q：為什麼這一點很重要呢？

A：企業執行委員會研究發現，上級決策者在做採購決策時最在意的第一件事情是團隊的一致支持。如果公司裡每個人對某一家供應商都有好的評語，那麼決策者就會選擇那一家供應商，而不是其他家。相反地，如果團隊中有些成員對於某家供應商有不好的評語，那麼決策者就可能選擇其他家，也就是獲得團隊較多支持的那一家。

Q：我懂了。所以跟客戶的所有員工、而不只是決策者建立關係是很重要的。

A：是的，簡單來說就是如此。

Unit 12

Coca Cola
可口可樂

學習重點 公司介紹

聽聽看

1 請聽一段關於可口可樂的公司介紹，你可以聽懂多少呢？在聽之前，請看看下列字彙，你覺得哪些字會出現在這段聽力中呢。 Track 32

- ☐ bottle 瓶
- ☐ choice 選擇
- ☐ fizzy 發泡的
- ☐ Olympics 奧運
- ☐ policy 政策
- ☐ secret 秘密
- ☐ soft drink 不含酒精飲料
- ☐ sugar 糖
- ☐ taste 味道
- ☐ unique 獨特的

小叮嚀

藉由這些單字提示，對你聽懂這段公司介紹是否有幫助呢？請在下列線段標示出你的理解程度，在本章最後，我們會再次做相同的評量，看看你進步了多少。

0% 10% 20% 30% 40% 50% 60% 70% 80% 90% 100%

聽聽看

2 請再聽一次公司介紹，以下陳述如果「正確」，請標示 T；「錯誤」者請標示 F。 Track 32

例	Coca-Cola 是世界上最大的飲料公司。	T
1	消費者愈來愈常看到他們的廣告。	
2	Coca-Cola 不被准許贊助 1994 世界盃。	
3	Coca-Cola 贊助過 1996 年亞特蘭大奧運。	
4	該公司做了不負責任的行銷。	
5	Coca-Cola 把廣告目標鎖定在兒童。	

6	該公司只生產一項產品。	
7	Coca-Cola Zero 是該公司史上最成功的產品之一。	
8	Coca-Cola 公司占了美國飲料市場的 41%。	

答案 請見 123 頁。

如果聽第一次時無法完全掌握上述訊息，請多練習幾次。接著，我們來學習介紹公司時會用到的字彙。

動動腦 3 連連看，請將下列字彙與正確意思配對。見範例。

responsible marketing policy	對他們健康有害
detrimental to their health	以……為直接行銷目標
make the right choices	做正確的選擇
marketing mediums	行銷媒介
targeted demographic tracking	產品推出；上市
direct targeting	責任行銷政策
product launches	目標族群統計追蹤

答案 請見 123 頁。核對完答案，請花點時間熟悉這些字彙，並跟著 CD 練習發音。 Track 33

請再回頭聽一次介紹，並留意上列字彙在上下文的使用方式，如有需要可以參閱本章末的 CD 內容，將聽力段落當成字彙的使用範文來學習。

這段公司介紹提及可口可樂的一些產品，我們來熟悉一下它們吧。

說說看 **4** 下列這些品牌，你認得幾個？請跟著 CD 練習它們的發音。 Track 34

	我認識的品牌請打勾
Barq's Root Beer 伯克沙士	
Caffeine-Free Diet Coke 無咖啡因健怡可樂	
Coca-Cola Classic 經典口味的可樂	
Diet Coke 健怡可樂	
Fruitopia 水果國（一種果汁補給飲料）	
Nestea 雀巢	
Powerade 動樂（一種運動飲料）	
Sprite 雪碧	

公司介紹中出現了 put into perspective 和 corner the market 這兩個俚語，我們來學習它們的用法。

動動腦 **5** 請勾選這二個俚語的正確解釋。

	put into perspective
	make a drawing
	make a comparison
	put something somewhere safe

	corner the market
	become market leader
	go for a drive
	go to the market and do some shopping

答案 如果摸不著頭緒，可以藉由聽力段落的上下文，判斷它們的意思為何。答案請見 123 頁。

公司介紹所提及的大都爲事實陳述，所以動詞大部分爲現在簡單式。下列動詞在談論公司時可以派上用場。

動動腦 6 連連看，請將動詞、動詞字串和正確解釋配對。

■ be applied to •	• 製造
■ be exposed to •	• 適用於……
■ be sold •	• 盡力去……
■ be well known for •	• 生產
■ make every attempt to •	• 採取
■ make •	• 被出售
■ operate •	• 以……而享盛名
■ produce •	• 利用
■ use •	• 暴露於……；可接觸到……

答案 請見 123 頁。

聽聽看 7 請再聽一次公司介紹，並以上一題的字串完成這些句子。 Track 32

1. It ____________ products that ____________ all over the world.

2. Coca-Cola ____________ unique and interesting advertising.

3. The company ____________ a responsible marketing policy.

4. Children __________ advertising.

5. Soft drink products may __________ their health.

6. The policy __________ all marketing mediums.

7. The Coca-Cola Company also __________ avoid direct targeting of children.

8. Coca-Cola __________ their soda Coca-Cola Classic.

9. They also __________ many other products.

答案 請見 124 頁。請留意主詞和動詞的一致性。

說說看

8 請使用你在本章學會的用語，為這段公司介紹做個摘要，並練習開口說。

小叮嚀

請把你的口說摘要錄音，並聽錄音評量自己的進步狀況。可以多練習幾次，直到可以說得流利。

聽聽看

9 最後請再聽一次公司介紹，並在下列線段標示出你的理解程度。經過一連串學習，你的聽力理解進步了嗎？如果沒有，請再回頭針對弱項加強。 Track 32

0% 10% 20% 30% 40% 50% 60% 70% 80% 90% 100%

解答

聽聽看 2

1. T
2. F，他們贊助過。
3. T
4. F，該公司採取的是責任行銷策略。
5. F，Coca-Cola 避免以孩子為直接的行銷目標。
6. F，他們生產許多種類的產品。
7. T
8. T

動動腦 3

responsible marketing policy	責任行銷政策
detrimental to their health	對他們健康有害
make the right choices	做正確的選擇
marketing mediums	行銷媒介
targeted demographic tracking	目標族群統計追蹤
direct targeting	以……為直接行銷目標
product launches	產品推出；上市

動動腦 5

put into perspective = **make a comparison** 做比較

corner the market = **become market leader** 成為市場領導者

動動腦 6

be applied to	適用於……
be exposed to	暴露於……；可接觸到……

be sold	被出售
be well known for	以……而享盛名
make every attempt to	盡力去……
make	製造
operate	採取
produce	生產
use	利用

聽聽看 7

1. It **makes** products that **are sold** all over the world.
2. Coca-Cola **uses** unique and interesting advertising.
3. The company **operates** a responsible marketing policy.
4. Children **are not exposed to** advertising.
5. Soft drink products may **be detrimental to** their health.
6. The policy **is applied to** all marketing mediums.
7. The Coca-Cola Company also **makes every attempt to** avoid direct targeting of children.
8. Coca-Cola **is well known for** their soda Coca-Cola Classic.
9. They also **produce** many other products.

CD 內容

Track 32

The Coca-Cola Company is the world's largest soft-drink company. It makes products that are sold all over the world, in over 190 countries. Coca-Cola uses unique and interesting advertising to increase sales, and consumers are becoming more and more exposed to their advertising. Coca-Cola sponsored the 1994 World Cup, as well as the 1996 Olympics in Atlanta. The company operates a responsible marketing policy which makes sure children are not exposed to advertising for soft drink products which may be detrimental to their health, and to help parents make the right choices for their kids. The policy is applied to all marketing mediums where targeted demographic tracking is available: television, radio, print, the Internet and mobile phones. The Coca-Cola Company also makes every attempt to avoid direct targeting of children in other areas where parents may not be present to supervise, such as schools.

Coca-Cola is well known for their soda Coca-Cola Classic, but they also produce many other products, such as Diet Coke, Caffeine-Free Diet Coke, Sprite, Nestea, Powerade, Barq's Root Beer, and Fruitopia. Coca-Cola Zero is one of the most successful product launches in the company's history. In the first year of launching, they sold nearly 450 million cases globally. Put into perspective, that's roughly the same size as their total business in the Philippines, one of their top 15 markets. As of September 2008, Coca-Cola Zero is available in more than 100 countries.

The Coca-Cola Company has cornered 41% of the US soft-drink market and 50% of the international soft-drink market.

【中譯】

Coca-Cola 公司是全世界最大的飲料公司，它製造的產品行銷全球超過 190 個國家。 Coca-Cola 利用獨特而有趣的廣告來增加銷售量，顧客們愈來愈常接觸到他們的廣告。 Coca-Cola 贊助過 1994 年世界盃，以及 1996 年的亞特蘭大奧運。公司採取的是責任行銷原則，確保兒童不會看到可能對他們健康有害的飲料產品廣告，而且幫助家長為他們的孩子做正確的選擇。這個原則適用於所有可以取得目標族群統計追蹤的行銷媒介：電視、廣播、印刷品、網路和手機。 Coca-Cola 公司也盡力在其他家長可能無法在場監督的地方，例如學校，避免以兒童為直接行銷目標。

Coca-Cola 最具盛名是他們經典口味的可樂汽水 (Coca-Cola Classic)，不過他們也生產許多其他產品，例如健怡可樂 (Diet Coke)、無咖啡因健怡可樂 (Caffeine-Free Diet Coke)、雪碧 (Sprite)、雀巢檸檬茶 (Nestea)、運動飲料 Powerade、伯克沙士 (Barq's Root Beer) 和果汁補給飲料 Frutiopia。零熱量的 Coca-Cola Zero 是這家公司有史以來最成功的上市產品之一，推出第一年全球即銷售了 4 億 5 千萬箱。對照來說，大概等於他們前 15 大市場之一菲律賓地區的總業績規模。直至 2008 年九月，在 100 多個國家都買得到 Coca-Cola Zero 了。

Coca-Cola 公司占了美國飲料市場的 41% 和全球飲料市場的 50%。

Unit 13

The Housing Market

房屋市場

學習重點 房市的市場趨勢

聽聽看

1 請聽一段美國房市的報導，你可以聽懂多少呢？在聽之前，請看看下列字彙，你覺得哪些字會出現在這段聽力中呢。 Track 35

- [ ] apartment 公寓
- [ ] furniture 家具
- [ ] garden 花園
- [ ] home 家
- [ ] house 房子
- [ ] market 市場
- [ ] price 價格
- [ ] sale 業績
- [ ] swimming pool 游泳池
- [ ] dog 狗

小叮嚀

藉由這些單字提示，對你聽懂這段報導是否有幫助呢？請在下列線段標示出你的理解程度，在本章最後，我們會再次做相同的評量，看看你進步了多少。

0% 10% 20% 30% 40% 50% 60% 70% 80% 90% 100%

聽聽看

2 請再聽一次報導，以下陳述如果「正確」，請標示 **T**；「錯誤」者請標示 **F**。 Track 35

例	現今住屋銷售量是近 12 年來的最低水平。	T
1	民眾愈來愈憂心經濟景氣。	
2	房屋售價提高。	
3	西部地區的房市表現特別差。	
4	平均房屋售價上漲。	
5	市場上有許多房貸抵押的法拍屋。	

6	將近一半的待售屋都是房貸抵押的法拍屋。	
7	這對買家來說是壞消息。	
8	歐巴馬總統要設法幫助首次購屋者。	

答案 請見 133 頁。

如果聽第一次時無法完全掌握上述訊息，請多練習幾次。接著，我們來學習談論房市時可以派上用場的字彙。

動動腦 **3 連連看，請將下列字彙與正確意思配對。見範例。**

housing market	可負擔的價格
annual rate	年率
weakest showing	平均售價
seasonal factors	扣押財產
nationwide sales	首次購（屋）者
average sales price	首次購屋者抵稅金額
swamping the market	房市
mortgage foreclosures	低利率
distressed properties	房貸抵押法拍屋
affordable prices	全國的銷售量
low interest rates	季節性因素
first-time homebuyer tax credit	市場上氾濫著……
first time buyers	最差的表現

答案 請見 133 頁。核對完答案，請花點時間熟悉這些字彙，並跟著 CD 練習發音。 Track 36

請再回頭聽一次報導，並留意上列字彙在上下文的使用方式，如有需要可以參閱本章末的CD內容，將聽力段落當成字彙的使用範文來學習。

這段報導中使用了幾個俚語，我們來學習它們的用法。

動動腦 **4** 請勾選下列二個用語的正確解釋。

	bottom out
	fall over
	reach the bottom of a hill
	stop falling

	swamp the market
	be a bad place
	fill the market with bad products
	fill the market with good products

答案 如果摸不著頭緒，可以藉由聽力段落的上下文，判斷它們的意思為何。答案請見134頁。

談論市場趨勢時，有一些經常使用的詞彙，在這段報導中也有出現。

動動腦 **5** 如果要將這些字串分為二類，你會怎麼分類？

- have unexpectedly plunged 無預期地下跌
- is growing 正在成長
- have fallen 已經下跌
- have gone down 已經下跌
- are waiting 正在等待
- are continuing 正在持續
- is showing 正在展示出

- has shrunk 已經減少
- are paying 正在支付
- are swamping 正充斥著
- is helping 正在幫助

答案 請見 134 頁。

分析

- 此報導描述的是房市目前的情況。
- 此兩類動詞字串都可用來描述目前情況：have + p.p. 動詞字串著重於現在的結果；be Ving 動詞字串則著重於目前的活動或趨勢，無關結果。

聽聽看

6 請再聽一次報導，並填上上一題字串所搭配的前後文。

Track 35

1. ______________ have unexpectedly plunged ______________
2. ______________________________ is growing.
3. ______________________________ are waiting.
4. ______________________________ have fallen.
5. ______________ are continuing ______________
6. ______________________________ have gone down.
7. ______________ is showing ______________
8. ______________________________ has shrunk.
9. ______________ are swamping ______________
10. ______________ are paying ______________
11. ______________ is helping ______________

答案 請見 134 頁。

說說看

7 請使用你在本章學會的用語，為這段報導做個摘要，並練習開口說。

小叮嚀

請把你的口說摘要錄音，並聽錄音評量自己的進步狀況。可以多練習幾次，直到可以說得流利。

聽聽看

8 最後請再聽一次報導，並在下列線段標示出你的理解程度。經過一連串學習，你的聽力理解進步了嗎？如果沒有，請再回頭針對弱項加強。 Track 35

0%	10%	20%	30%	40%	50%	60%	70%	80%	90%	100%

解答

聽聽看 2

1. T
2. F，售價持續下跌。
3. F，西部是全國唯一銷售量增加的地區。
4. F，平均售價下跌。
5. T
6. T
7. F，這對買家來說是好消息。
8. T

動動腦 3

housing market	房市
annual rate	年率
weakest showing	最差的表現
seasonal factors	季節性因素
nationwide sales	全國的銷售量
average sales price	平均售價
swamping the market	市場上氾濫著……
mortgage foreclosures	房貸抵押法拍屋
distressed properties	扣押財產
affordable prices	可負擔的價格
low interest rates	低利率
first-time homebuyer tax credit	首次購屋者抵稅金額
first time buyers	首次購（屋）者

動動腦 4

bottom out = **stop falling** 停止下跌

swamp the market = **fill the market with bad products** 劣質產品充斥市場

動動腦 5

這些動詞字串可以分成兩類：

- **have + p.p.** 動詞字串：have unexpectedly plunged、have fallen、has shrunk、have gone down
- **be Ving** 動詞字串：is growing、are waiting、are continuing、is showing、are swamping、are paying、is helping

聽聽看 6

1. **Sales of existing homes** have unexpectedly plunged **to the lowest level**.
2. **Pessimism about the economy** is growing.
3. **Buyers** are waiting.
4. **Sales of existing homes** have fallen.
5. **Prices** are continuing **to sink**.
6. **Nationwide sales** have gone down.
7. **The West** is showing **increased sales**.
8. **The average sales price** has shrunk.
9. **Mortgage foreclosures** are swamping **the market**.
10. **Buyers** are paying **the most affordable prices in years**.
11. **The first-time homebuyer tax credit** is helping **to make the market more attractive**.

CD 内容

Track 35

Sales of existing homes have unexpectedly plunged to the lowest level in nearly 12 years as pessimism about the economy is growing and buyers are waiting for President Barack Obama's plan to help revive the U.S. housing market.

Sales of existing homes have fallen 5.3 percent to an annual rate of 4.49 million, from 4.74 million in December. This is the weakest showing since July 1997, and some analysts don't see sales bottoming out until later this year as prices are continuing to sink.

Without adjusting for seasonal factors, nationwide sales have gone down 7.6 percent from a year earlier. The West is the only part of the U.S. which is showing increased sales.

The average sales price has shrunk to $170,300, down 14.8 percent from $199,800 a year earlier and from $175,000 in December. This is the lowest price since March 2003 and the second-largest drop on record.

Mortgage foreclosures are swamping the market — especially in particularly distressed states like California, Florida, Nevada and Arizona. The Realtors group estimates that about 45 percent of sales nationwide are foreclosures or other distressed properties.

That's great news for buyers, who are paying the most affordable prices in years. Also, the combination of low interest rates and the $8,000 first-time homebuyer tax credit introduced by President Obama is helping to make the market more attractive for first time buyers.

【中譯】

由於對經濟景氣日益悲觀，買家們都在等待歐巴馬總統協助振興美國房市的方案，現今的住屋銷售意外跌至近 12 年來的最低水平。

現有住房的年銷售量下挫了百分之 5.3 ，從十二月的 474 萬來到 449 萬。這是自 1997 年七月以來最差的表現，因為房價仍在持續重挫，有些分析師認為要到今年年底銷售量才會觸底反彈。

在未調整季節因素的情況下，全國銷售量比去年減少百分之 7.6 。西部是美國唯一出現銷售量增長的地區。

平均售價從去年的 19 萬 9 千 8 百美元下跌至 17 萬零 3 百美元，跌了百分之 14.8 ，十二月份則是 17 萬 5 千美元。這是自 2003 年三月以來的最低房價，也是歷史上第二大跌幅。

市場上房貸抵押法拍屋氾濫——尤其是在特別困頓的幾個州，如：加州、佛羅里達、內華達和亞利桑納。房地產集團 Realtors 估計全國百分之 45 的住屋銷售都是房貸抵押或其他扣押財產法拍屋。

這對買家來說是大好消息，他們支付的是多年來最實惠的價格。而且，歐巴馬總統所推行的低利率和首次購屋者 8 千美元抵稅金額的整合配套也有助於讓市場吸引更多首次購屋者。

Unit 14

US Stocks Down

美國股市下跌

學習重點 股市行情

聽聽看

1 請聽一段美國股市的報導，你可以聽懂多少呢？在聽之前，請看看下列字彙，你覺得哪些字會出現在這段聽力中呢。 Track 37

- ☐ average 平均
- ☐ bear 熊
- ☐ corporate 公司的
- ☐ dollar 美元
- ☐ personal 個人的
- ☐ post office 郵局
- ☐ river 河
- ☐ sector 產業
- ☐ stock 股票
- ☐ tax 稅

小叮嚀

藉由這些單字提示，對你聽懂這段報導是否有幫助呢？請在下列線段標示出你的理解程度，在本章最後，我們會再次做相同的評量，看看你進步了多少。

○—○—○—○—○—○—○—○—○—○—○

0% 10% 20% 30% 40% 50% 60% 70% 80% 90% 100%

聽聽看

2 請再聽一次報導，以下陳述如果「正確」，請標示 **T**；「錯誤」者請標示 **F**。 Track 37

例	這個消息對美國股票市場不利。	T
1	AIG 發生了美國企業史上最大的虧損。	
2	Buffett 說他的公司第四季出現獲利。	
3	道瓊指數跌破了 7,000 點的關卡。	
4	標準普爾 500 指數跌破了 700 點關卡。	
5	納斯達克指數下跌。	

6	原油期貨交易上漲。	
7	個人所得提高。	
8	個人消費降低。	
9	國家儲蓄率提高。	

答案 請見 145 頁。

如果聽第一次時無法完全掌握上述訊息，請多練習幾次。接著，我們來學習談論股市時可以派上用場的字彙。

動動腦 **3 連連看，請將下列字彙與正確意思配對。見範例。**

■ ongoing worries •	• 比預期的好
■ global economy •	• 建設支出
■ financial sector •	• 悲觀的評論
■ downbeat comments •	• 經濟報導
■ latest round of selling •	• 金融產業
■ unending stream •	• 全球經濟
■ government aid •	• 政府援助
■ operating company •	• 主要的股市指數
■ key market indexes •	• 最近一波的拋售
■ overall trading •	• 持續的擔心
■ better than expected •	• 經營的公司
■ economic reports •	• 整體交易
■ personal income •	• 個人消費
■ personal consumption •	• 個人所得
■ savings rate •	• 儲蓄率
■ construction spending •	• 永無止境的一連串……

答案 請見145頁。核對完答案，請花點時間熟悉這些字彙，並跟著CD練習發音。 Track 38

數字是股市行情中不可或缺的重要訊息，我們再來熟悉它們的唸法。

說說看 **4 請跟著CD練習這些數字的發音。** Track 39

- $61.7 billion
- 500
- 4.24%
- 3.99%
- 0.4%
- 3.3%
- $30 billion
- 700
- 6,763.29
- 1,322.85
- 0.6%
- 7,000
- 299.64 points
- 34.27 points
- 29
- 5.0%

在報導中也提及幾個美國重要的股票指數和交易所，認識它們對於談論美國股市行情或閱讀財經新聞都有幫助。

說說看 **5 請跟著CD練習這些股票指數和交易所的發音。** Track 40

- The Nasdaq Composite Index 納斯達克綜合指數
- Dow Jones Industrial Average 道瓊工業平均指數
- The Dollar Index 美元指數
- New York Stock Exchange 紐約股票交易所
- S&P 500 Index 標準普爾500指數

接著來認識一些不同類型的股票名稱。

動動腦 **6** 連連看，請將下列字彙與正確中譯配對。見範例。

■ stocks •	• 原油期貨
■ treasuries •	• 黃金期貨
■ gold futures •	• 股票
■ crude oil futures •	• 公債

答案 請見 146 頁。核對完答案，請跟著 CD 練習它們的唸法。 Track 41

在這段股市報導中，使用了幾個特殊詞彙，我們來學習它們的用法。

動動腦 **7** 請勾選下列三個詞彙的正確解釋。

	spark
	start a fire
	start an engine
	be the cause of sth.

	shambles
	moving badly
	a disorganized situation
	a strange place

	pay little heed to
	pay some money to sb.
	a kind of tax
	ignore sth.

答案 如果摸不著頭緒，可以藉由聽力段落的上下文，判斷它們的意思為何。答案請見 146 頁。

動動腦

8 下列是用來描述股票市場向上或向下走勢的字串，如果要分成三類，你會怎麼分類？

- closed sharply 收盤大幅（走低或走高）
- a record loss 有史以來最大的虧損
- posted the largest loss 公布最大的虧損
- posted a huge fourth-quarter loss 公布第四季的巨大虧損
- slump 崩盤；重挫
- were at multi-year lows（收盤）在多年來的新低點
- lost 減少；下降
- shed 下掉；減少
- was lower 更少；減少
- were higher 更多；上漲
- fell 下跌；減少
- slumped 重挫；暴跌
- rose 提高；增加
- a five year low 五年來的新低

答案 請見 146 頁。核對完答案，請花點時間熟悉這些字串並跟著 CD 練習它們的唸法。 Track 42

聽聽看

9 請再聽一次報導，並用上一題字串來完成這些句子。

Track 37

1. US stocks __________ and broadly lower.
2. News of __________ from AIG sparked the latest round of selling.
3. AIG __________ in U.S. corporate history.
4. The operating company __________.
5. Monday's __________ sent the Dow Jones industrial average below the 7,000 level.
6. Other key market indexes __________.
7. The 30-stock Dow Jones industrial average __________ 299.64 points.
8. The broad S&P 500 index __________ 34.27 points.
9. The tech-heavy Nasdaq composite index __________ by 54.99 points.
10. Treasuries __________.
11. Gold futures __________.
12. Crude oil futures __________ on demand worries.
13. Personal income __________ 0.4%.
14. February construction spending fell by a more than expected 3.3% to __________.

答案 請見 147 頁。請留意這些字串在上下文的使用方式。

說說看

10 請使用你在本章學會的用語，為這段報導做個摘要，並練習開口說。

小叮嚀

請把你的口說摘要錄音，並聽錄音評量自己的進步狀況。可以多練習幾次，直到可以說得流利。

聽聽看

11 最後請再聽一次報導，並在下列線段標示出你的理解程度。經過一連串學習，你的聽力理解進步了嗎？如果沒有，請再回頭針對弱項加強。 Track 37

0% 10% 20% 30% 40% 50% 60% 70% 80% 90% 100%

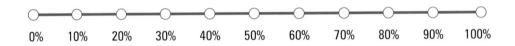

解答

聽聽看 2

1. T
2. F，Buffett 說他的公司第四季出現虧損。
3. T
4. F，標準普爾 500 指數剛好守住 700 點關卡。
5. T
6. F，原油期貨交易重挫。
7. T
8. F，個人消費提高。
9. T

動動腦 3

ongoing worries	持續的擔心
global economy	全球經濟
financial sector	金融產業
downbeat comments	悲觀的評論
latest round of selling	最近一波的拋售
unending stream	永無止盡的一連串……
government aid	政府援助
operating company	經營的公司
key market indexes	主要的股市指數
overall trading	整體交易
better than expected	比預期的好
economic reports	經濟報導
personal income	個人所得
personal consumption	個人消費

savings rate	儲蓄率
construction spending	建設支出

動動腦 6

stocks	股票
treasuries	公債
gold futures	黃金期貨
crude oil futures	原油期貨

動動腦 7

- spark = **be the cause of sth.** 成為……的導火線
- shambles = **a disorganized situation** 混亂的情況
- pay little heed to = **ignore sth.** 忽略……

動動腦 8

可分為三類：

- 動詞：lost、shed、slumped、rose、fell
- 名詞：a record loss、slump、a five year low
- 其他如「動詞 + 名詞」或「動詞 + 形容詞／副詞」的組合：closed sharply、posted the largest loss、posted a huge fourth-quarter loss、were at multi-year lows、was lower、were higher

聽聽看 9

1. US stocks **closed sharply** and broadly lower.
2. News of **a record loss** from AIG sparked the latest round of selling.
3. AIG **posted the largest loss** in U.S. corporate history.
4. The operating company **posted a huge fourth-quarter loss**.

5. Monday's **slump** sent the Dow Jones industrial average below the 7,000 level.
6. Other key market indexes **were at multi-year lows**.
7. The 30-stock Dow Jones industrial average **lost** 299.64 points.
8. The broad S&P 500 index **shed** 34.27 points.
9. The tech-heavy Nasdaq composite index **was lower** by 54.99 points.
10. Treasuries **were higher**.
11. Gold futures **fell**.
12. Crude oil futures **slumped** on demand worries.
13. Personal income **rose** 0.4%.
14. February construction spending fell by a more than expected 3.3% to **a five year low**.

CD 内容

Track 37

US stocks closed sharply and broadly lower on Monday, impacted by investors' ongoing worries about the global economy and financial sector. News of a record loss from AIG and downbeat comments from investing icon Warren Buffett sparked the latest round of selling.

The seemingly unending stream of bad news from the financial sector continued Monday. This time, it was word that AIG posted the largest loss in U.S. corporate history — losses amounting to $61.7 billion — and will receive $30 billion in government aid.

Meanwhile, legendary investor Buffett said the U.S. economy is in a "shambles;" his operating company posted a huge fourth-quarter loss.

Monday's slump sent the Dow Jones industrial average below the 7,000 level for the first time since 1997. Other key market indexes were at multi-year lows as well, with the S&P 500 index barely holding above the 700 level.

On Monday, the 30-stock Dow Jones industrial average lost 299.64 points, or 4.24%, to 6,763.29. The broad S&P 500 index shed 34.27 points, or 4.66%, to 700.82. The tech-heavy Nasdaq composite index was lower by 54.99 points, or 3.99%, at 1,322.85. Overall trading was overwhelmingly negative, with 29 stocks lower in price on the New York

Stock Exchange for every two that gained.

Treasuries were higher, as was the dollar index. Gold futures fell. Crude oil futures slumped on demand worries.

However, it is not all bad news. Investors paid little heed Monday to some better than expected economic reports: January personal income rose 0.4%; personal consumption surprisingly rose 0.6%; the nation's savings rate rose 5.0%; February construction spending fell by a more than expected 3.3% to a five year low.

【中譯】

受到投資者持續擔憂全球經濟和金融產業的衝擊，美國股市週一收盤廣泛大幅走低。美國AIG出現有史以來最大虧損的消息和投資大師Warren Buffett看跌的評論引發了最近一波的拋售。

金融產業似乎無止境的一連串壞消息在週一繼續傳出。這一次，消息指出AIG公布了美國企業歷史上最大虧損——虧損金額高達617億美元——而且將獲得政府300億美元的援助。

於此同時，投資之神Buffett說，美國經濟現在是一個「爛攤子」；他經營的公司公布了第四季的巨額虧損。

週一的崩盤造成道瓊工業平均指數跌破7,000點關卡，是1997年以來的頭一遭。其他主要股市指數也都在多年來的新低點，標準普爾500指數幾乎守不住700點關卡。

週一，30日股票道瓊斯工業平均指數減少了299.64點，也就是4.24% ，來到6763.29點。標準普爾500指數掉了34.27點，也就是4.66% ，來到700.82點。以科技股為主的納斯達克綜合指數少了54.99點，也就是3.99% ，收盤在1322.85點。整體交易大幅走低，在紐約證券交易所每29支股票價格下跌，只有兩支上漲。

公債上漲，美元指數也是。黃金期貨交易走跌，原油期貨交易因需求擔憂造成重挫。

不過，也不全然都是壞消息。投資人在週一幾乎都沒注意到這些比預期來得正面的經濟報導：一月份的個人所得提高了0.4% ；個人消費出乎意外提高了0.6% ；國家儲蓄率提高5.0% ；二月份的建設支出降低3.3% ，超出預期，是五年來的新低。

Unit
15

Growth in Network Service Market

網路服務市場的成長

學習重點 電信業的市場趨勢（英國口音）

聽聽看

1 請聽一段關於 AT&T 未來計畫的報導，AT&T 是美國最大的有線、無線網路暨手機用戶服務提供商。你可以聽懂多少呢？在聽之前，請看看下列字彙，你覺得哪些字會出現在這段聽力中呢。 Track 43

- ☐ application 應用
- ☐ cable 電纜
- ☐ city 城市
- ☐ entertainment 娛樂
- ☐ internet 網際
- ☐ modem 數據機
- ☐ network 網路
- ☐ news 新聞
- ☐ service 服務
- ☐ wireless 無線

小叮嚀

藉由這些單字提示，對你聽懂這段報導是否有幫助呢？請在下列線段標示出你的理解程度，在本章最後，我們會再次做相同的評量，看看你進步了多少。

0% 10% 20% 30% 40% 50% 60% 70% 80% 90% 100%

聽聽看

2 請再聽一次報導，以下陳述如果「正確」，請標示 T；「錯誤」者請標示 F。 Track 43

例	AT&T 有一些好消息。	T
1	AT&T 今年將會削減 3,000 個工作機會。	
2	他們將會擴大無線和寬頻的收訊範圍。	
3	他們將會削減其他領域的 12,000 個工作機會。	
4	工作削減將從十二月開始。	
5	網路上的資料傳輸量減少。	

6	他們今年會把 3G 手機寬頻服務擴展到 20 個新市場。	
7	公司的股票據估會下跌。	

答案 請見 157 頁。

如果聽第一次時無法完全掌握上述訊息，請多練習幾次。接著，我們來學習談論電信業時可以派上用場的字彙。

動動腦 **3 連連看，請將下列字彙與正確意思配對。見範例。**

■ broadband networks •	• 寬頻網路
■ provide coverage •	• 寬頻服務
■ broadband services •	• 基地台
■ tough economy •	•（股市）收盤價
■ wireless networks •	• 資料傳輸量
■ new applications •	• 手機寬頻服務
■ data traffic •	• 新的應用
■ third-generation •	• 提供（收訊）範圍
■ mobile broadband service •	• 第三代
■ cell sites •	• 艱困的經濟
■ closing price •	• 無線網路

答案 請見 157 頁。核對完答案，請花點時間熟悉這些字彙，並跟著 CD 練習發音。 Track 44

這段報導也提及了一些數字資訊，我們來練習它們的唸法。

說說看 4 請跟著 CD 練習這些數字的發音。 Track 45

- 3,000
- 12,000
- 20
- $23.02
- $17 billion
- 4 percent
- $1.30
- $18 billion
- 50 percent
- 6 percent

接著我們來學習這段報導中使用的二個特殊詞彙。

動動腦 5 請勾選下列二個用語的正確解釋。

	a shift toward sth.
	a general trend
	working for a set number of hours

	embrace sth.
	kiss and hug someone
	start using a new product or service enthusiastically

答案 如果摸不著頭緒，可以藉由聽力段落的上下文，判斷它們的意思為何。答案請見 157 頁。

這段報導談論的是 AT&T 的未來計畫，所以出現了許多可以用來說明未來趨勢的字串。

說說看 6 請跟著 CD 練習這些談論未來字串的說法。

Track 46

- are forecast to V 據預測會……
- has plans to V 有計畫……
- is going to V 將會……
- plans on Ving 有……方面的計畫
- predicted at 預測為……
- expects to V 預期……
- look certain to V 看來肯定會……
- look set to V 看來預計會……
- plans to V 計畫要……
- will V 將會……

聽聽看 7 請再聽一次報導，並以上一題的字串完成這些句子。

Track 43

1. It ___________ add nearly 3,000 jobs.
2. It ___________ invest $17 billion.
3. It ___________ add jobs in 2009.
4. It still ___________ cut jobs.
5. AT&T said it ___________ cutting 12,000 jobs.
6. The job cuts ___________ continue.
7. AT&T said it ___________ expand its third-generation service.
8. It ___________ expand in Oklahoma.
9. Shares of the company ___________ gain $1.30.
10. A closing price ___________ $23.02.

答案 請見 158 頁。

說說看

8 請使用你在本章學會的用語，為這段報導做個摘要，並練習開口說。

小叮嚀

請把你的口說摘要錄音，並聽錄音評量自己的進步狀況。可以多練習幾次，直到可以說得流利。

聽聽看

9 最後請再聽一次報導，並在下列線段標示出你的理解程度。經過一連串學習，你的聽力理解進步了嗎？如果沒有，請再回頭針對弱項加強。 Track 43

0% 10% 20% 30% 40% 50% 60% 70% 80% 90% 100%

解答

聽聽看 2

1. **F**，他們今年會增加近 3,000 個工作機會。
2. **T**
3. **T**
4. **F**，去年十二月就開始了。
5. **F**，是增加的。
6. **T**
7. **F**，據估會上漲。

動動腦 3

broadband networks	寬頻網路
provide coverage	提供（收訊）範圍
broadband services	寬頻服務
tough economy	艱困的經濟
wireless networks	無線網路
new applications	新的應用
data traffic	資料傳輸量
third-generation	第三代
mobile broadband service	手機寬頻服務
cell sites	基地台
closing price	（股市）收盤價

動動腦 5

- a shift toward sth. = **a general trend** ……的趨勢
- embrace sth. = **start using a new product or service enthusiastically**
  熱切地採用……

聽聽看 7

1. It **will** add nearly 3,000 jobs.
2. It **is going to** invest $17 billion.
3. It **plans to** add jobs in 2009.
4. It still **expects to** cut jobs.
5. AT&T said it **plans on** cutting 12,000 jobs.
6. The job cuts **look set to** continue.
7. AT&T said it **looks certain to** expand its third-generation service.
8. It **has plans to** expand in Oklahoma.
9. Shares of the company **are forecast to** gain $1.30.
10. A closing price **predicted at** $23.02.

CD 內容

Track 43

It is not all bad news on the economy. AT&T Inc. announced on Tuesday that it will add nearly 3,000 jobs this year and is going to invest between $17 billion and $18 billion to drive growth by enhancing wireless and broadband networks in order to provide more coverage.

AT&T said it plans to add jobs in 2009 to meet continued demand for broadband services, but still expects to cut jobs in other areas, as previously announced, because of a tough economy and a shift toward wireless networks and broadband.

In December, AT&T said it plans on cutting 12,000 jobs, or about 4 percent of its work force. The job cuts began in December and look set to continue throughout 2009.

"Demand for broadband continues to grow as new applications emerge and customers embrace them, leading to data traffic on our network growing more than 50 percent year-over-year on average," said Chief Executive Randall Stephenson.

AT&T said it looks certain to expand its third-generation, or 3G, mobile broadband service to 20 new markets this year. The company also said it has plans to expand in Oklahoma by adding at least 30 new cell sites in the state this year, in Oklahoma City, Tulsa and Shawnee, among other cities.

Shares of the company are forecast to gain $1.30, or 6 percent, with a closing price predicted at $23.02.

【中譯】

經濟方面並不全然是壞消息。AT&T Inc. 星期二宣布，為了促進成長，今年將增加近 3,000 個工作機會，並投資 170 億到 180 億美元來增強無線和寬頻網絡，提供更大的收訊範圍。

AT&T 表示 2009 年計畫增加工作機會，滿足寬頻服務的持續需求，但是如先前所宣布，因為艱困的經濟條件和轉換成無線網路和寬頻的趨勢，預期仍會削減其他領域的工作機會。

在十二月，AT&T 表示計畫削減 12,000 個工作機會，大約公司人力的 4%。工作削減自十二月開始，預計會持續到整個 2009 年。

執行長 Randall Stephenson 說：「寬頻的需求持續增加，因為新的應用出現，消費者也熱切接受，造成我們的網絡資料傳輸量平均每年增長 50% 以上。」

AT&T 表示，看來今年確定會把第三代手機寬頻服務，所謂 3G，擴展到 20 個新市場。公司也表示有計畫要在俄克拉荷馬州擴展市場，今年至少會在全州增加 30 個新的基地台，包括奧克拉荷馬市、土爾沙、肖尼和其他城市。

公司股票據估將增加 1.30 美元，或百分之 6，預測收盤價為 23.02 美元。

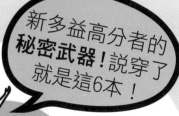

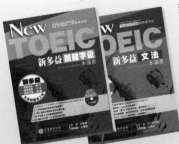

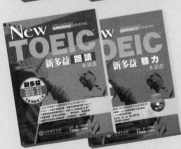

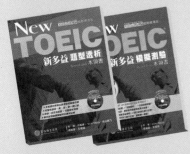

國家圖書館出版品預行編目資料

職場英文進化術. 菁英篇 / Quentin Brand 作； 陳玉娥譯.
-- 初版. -- 臺北市：貝塔出版：智勝文化發行, 2009. 09
面； 公分

ISBN 978-957-729-757-0（平裝附光碟片）

1. 商業英文 2. 讀本

805.18 98013914

職場英文進化術——菁英篇

作　　者 / Quentin Brand
譯　　者 / 陳玉娥
執行編輯 / 陳家仁

出　　版 / 貝塔出版有限公司
地　　址 / 台北市 100 館前路 12 號 11 樓
電　　話 / (02) 2314-2525
傳　　真 / (02) 2312-3535
客服專線 / (02) 2314-3535
客服信箱 / btservice@betamedia.com.tw
郵撥帳號 / 19493777
帳戶名稱 / 貝塔出版有限公司

總 經 銷 / 時報文化出版企業股份有限公司
地　　址 / 桃園縣龜山鄉萬壽路二段 351 號
電　　話 / (02) 2306-6842

出版日期 / 2009 年 9 月初版一刷
定　　價 / 220 元
ISBN：978-957-729-757-0

喚醒你的英文語感！

對折後釘好，直接寄回即可！

廣 告 回 信
北區郵政管理局登記證
北台字第14256號
免 貼 郵 票

100 台北市中正區館前路12號11樓

貝塔語言出版 收

Beta Multimedia Publishing

寄件者住址 □□□

貝塔語言出版
Beta Multimedia Publishing
讀者服務專線（02）2314-3535　讀者服務傳真（02）2312-353
客戶服務信箱 btservice@betamedia.com.tw
www.betamedia.com.tw

謝謝您購買本書！！

貝塔語言擁有最優良之英文學習書籍，為提供您最佳的英語學習資訊，您可填妥此表後寄回（免貼郵票）將可不定期收到本公司最新發行書訊及活動訊息！

姓名：______________________ 性別：☐男 ☐女 生日：_____年_____月_____日

電話：(公)___________________(宅)___________________(手機)__________________

電子信箱：____

學歷：☐高中職含以下 ☐專科 ☐大學 ☐研究所含以上

職業：☐金融 ☐服務 ☐傳播 ☐製造 ☐資訊 ☐軍公教 ☐出版

☐自由 ☐教育 ☐學生 ☐其他

職級：☐企業負責人 ☐高階主管 ☐中階主管 ☐職員 ☐專業人士

1. 您購買的書籍是？__________________________________

2. 您從何處得知本產品？(可複選)

☐書店 ☐網路 ☐書展 ☐校園活動 ☐廣告信函 ☐他人推薦 ☐新聞報導 ☐其他

3. 您覺得本產品價格：

☐偏高 ☐合理 ☐偏低

4. 請問目前您每週花了多少時間學英語？

☐ 不到十分鐘 ☐ 十分鐘以上，但不到半小時 ☐ 半小時以上，但不到一小時

☐ 一小時以上，但不到兩小時 ☐ 兩個小時以上 ☐ 不一定

5. 通常在選擇語言學習書時，哪些因素是您會考慮的？

☐ 封面 ☐ 內容、實用性 ☐ 品牌 ☐ 媒體、朋友推薦 ☐ 價格☐ 其他________

6. 市面上您最需要的語言書種類為？

☐ 聽力 ☐ 閱讀 ☐ 文法 ☐ 口說 ☐ 寫作 ☐ 其他___________

7. 通常您會透過何種方式選購語言學習書籍？

☐ 書店門市 ☐ 網路書店 ☐ 郵購 ☐ 直接找出版社 ☐ 學校或公司團購

☐ 其他______________

8. 給我們的建議：____

____

喚醒你的英文語感！

Get a Feel for English !

喚醒你的英文語感！

Get a Feel for English !